Sowing the Seeds

Chris Leckonby

Sowing the Seeds

Collected Stories

Sowing the Seeds Collected Stories
ISBN 978 1 74027 978 9
Copyright © Chris Leckonby 2015
The ideas which gave rise to these stories were generated by real-life
situations; however, any apparent reference to specific individuals is purely
coincidental. The stories are entirely fictional.

First published separately as *Once Bitten* 2010, *Out of the Frypan* 2011
and *The Real World* 2013

This edition published 2015 by
GINNINDERRA PRESS
PO Box 3461 Port Adelaide SA 5015
www.ginninderrapress.com.au

Contents

Once Bitten

Dominic Pellegrino was a wide boy, a gangster with an illicit grog enterprise, who had already spent five of his thirty years in jail and was looking for more. He was swarthy, dark, sexy in a scruffy sort of way, with long ringlets almost down to his belly-button. He had a buxom blonde in tow, twenty-seven-year-old Betty 'boom-boom' Silvester, who had worldwide contacts in a drugs, booze and fags smuggling ring. (Her generous buttocks were the reason for the nickname, which began as 'bum-bum' until one bloke who called her that ended up in hospital less than a man, but she thought 'boom-boom' was cool.) Dominic had it made, as she was good both in bed and in business.

Dominic and Boom-boom, real name Agnes Goldsmith, were cruising around on his Harley in the sleepy hamlet of Once Bitten, where they had rented a large shed from which to conduct their nefarious goings-on. As they approached the shed, they came upon one Angus Stewart Wallace, a retired Scottish doctor out walking his golden retriever, Pistol. They gave each other a look, as best you can on a motorbike without falling off. The look said, 'He'd better just walk on by and not go snooping or…' Angus changed his mind about investigating the tell-tale marijuana odour emanating faintly from the shed…until another time. Dominic and Boom-boom cruised on.

Angus was staying at the Beer and Skittles until he found suitable lodgings. 'Retired' was a euphemism for 'struck off', as his skills and integrity had disintegrated since he succumbed to dope, in addition to his predilection for cigars and whisky. Booze and fags he could get at the pub, and now he was sure he'd found a source of dope. Pistol had strained embarrassingly at the leash as they walked past the shed, and he didn't want Dom and Boom-boom smelling a rat. He walked on, and came to the pretty rose-entwined cottage of Florence Whitehead, the Sunday school teacher, pillar of sobriety, the church and the community.

Seventy-year-old Florence was a spinster, her medical-student fiancé having been killed by a drunk driver when he was twenty-one. Her cats, her garden and her church work were her life…almost.

On Florence's garden gate was a small printed notice: 'Bed & Breakfast for sober single or couple. No pets or children. Terms negotiable.' Oh well, he'd see. He was good at disguising his habits. He walked up the crazy-paving path and rang the doorbell. Pistol knew better than to even look at her cats.

Florence came to the door and said 'Yes?' with the safety chain still fastened.

'Good afternoon. My name is Wallace. I'm looking for lodgings.'

He could have been anybody, but, having hidden her whisky, Florence opened the door, smelling money. Wallace. That was Angus's name! Pull yourself together, it's a common name, he's been dead fifty years… She nearly fainted when she saw him. It can't be, don't be silly. Could be his brother…

Angus left Pistol tied up on the porch and went in. Over afternoon tea, they discussed terms and conditions. Then came the paperwork. Full name…

She knew. Why had word got to her that he was dead? Had he recognised her? Of course she'd changed her name when she moved here, a new identity helping her to live with her bereavement. Her whole life since had been a lie.

Angus moved in. Two days later he returned to the shed for a snoop. Weekdays, Dom and Boom-boom were busy in the city. Casing the shed, Pistol became agitated, whining and pawing at the base of the door. Desperate for a joint by now, Angus was sorely tempted to break in, but had no idea how to do it and get away with it. There was marijuana in that shed. He went around the back, and piled up some logs to climb on to give him a look through a dirty window. No clue as to the shed's use was visible, but, to anyone passing in the lane, he was. A second door was barricaded on the inside.

He went away to think. Next day he returned, unfortunately just as

Dominic, sans Boom-boom, popped back to retrieve his camera. He'd left it there Sunday, and it was full of pornographic shots of Boom-boom. Sure he'd locked the shed, but…bloody hell, there's that bloke with the gundog that was here Sunday…

'What do you want?'

'Just out walking. Who wants to know?'

'You're trespassing! Get out of here!'

'OK, OK, no harm intended. What's to get excited about? I'm going!'

Pistol didn't like Dominic and let out a low growl until checked by Angus. He could read people better than Angus could by a country mile.

Dom got his camera, but he was flustered and preoccupied. What if… That bloke would have to go. He shadowed him back to the cottage. Aha, Florence! This was a job for Boom-boom.

Back in the city, he related his experience. "What I need you to do, honey," he wheedled, "is go see Florence. We know about her grog and fags. I'm sure you can bribe or blackmail her to cooperate. She's done it before, you know."

She'd have to go when Angus was out, as advertised by the presence or otherwise of Pistol chained by the front door. Florence's cats were the only non-humans allowed in the cottage.

"Miss Whitehead, may I come in? My name's Agnes Goldsmith and I…' (with a self-conscious smile) 'would like to talk business.'

Agnes was dressed down for the occasion, and Florence imagined her to be another potential B&B client.

'I'm sorry, I just took a permanent resident. I should have taken the notice down.'

"No, it's not that. Look, may I come in? I promise I'm not selling anything.'

Puzzled, intrigued, Florence let her in.

'It's about your guest that I want to see you…' Agnes alias Boom-boom put her case.

Florence's eyes widened, shocked, horrified…then she began to succumb to greed, and anger, heartbreak and frustration over what

Angus had done to her all those years ago. She was sure he still didn't know who she was, but of course he had not seen, and would never again see, the birthmark on her left buttock. She'd killed before and got away with it, and ten thousand pounds was not to be knocked back lightly. Besides, her reputation… If this girl really did know, and spilled the beans, Florence's life here was over.

'You leave me no choice,' she told Boom-boom, after an indecently short pause for thought. 'But…what guarantees do I have? How do I know you're genuine?'

'Think about it, Florence dear. If I'm for real, you gain ten thousand pounds, or lose your cred in Once Bitten. Why would I bother to come to you, a stranger, if I'm not?'

Angus returned late from his walk. He'd been to look at the shed again, and couldn't believe what he found. Someone had been in; the door was swinging in the breeze. Had Dom been careless when retrieving his camera? Who knew or cared? Help yourself to the dope, Angus, then report it to the police and go home via the Beer and Skittles for your usual.

Florence greeted him with a smile. 'Mr Wallace,' she said, 'I know you've been at the pub. It's OK: I drink too, but nobody knows. If you'd like to share one with me any time, it will be just our secret.'

Something about her demeanour, her body language, a tell-tale remainder of a former accent, bothered him but he couldn't place it at all.

That evening after dinner she got out the whisky and poured two doubles, her back to him just like in the whodunits.

'Angus,' she made bold, as they were not yet on first-name terms, 'you obviously don't know who I am.'

Angus's turn to almost faint. His wife had divorced him when she found out about his habits, and he'd gone short in the bedroom department for many years. Maybe he could invent some story, kiss and make up, start again with Florence… He downed his potion in one gulp and hugged Florence to him. He was well on his way to seeing that birthmark again when he lost consciousness.

It was all too much in one day for the local police, cracking an international drug ring and having a body on their hands, the body no less of the man who had reported the marijuana.

'He was such an old soak,' Florence told them. 'He had a heart attack. He came home full of grog and I could tell he'd been smoking dope, though goodness knows where he got it. He stank of cigars, would've smoked himself to death before long.'

Poor Florence. Angus dead, her boozy secret out, and she never got her money. But the glass was only half empty. She got away with murder.

Boot Camp

When I was a student at Mineralton Primary, it was the custom in Year 6 to study the history and geology of mining in South Australia, and if that sounds rather dry for a bunch of eleven-year-olds, well, you didn't know our teacher. Mrs Prescott was the coolest being ever to be in charge of a classroom, and we learned by doing; her maxim was 'When I hear, I forget. When I see, I remember. When I do, I understand', and life was all about practical experiments, drama, excursions and artwork. The culmination was a camp at Kalaroonta, in the heart of what used to be copper-mining territory.

My best friend, Jessica Parker, had her sights on becoming Australia's best-selling living novelist. She was adventurous, brainy, wore a hearing aid and was given to 'romancing'. She wouldn't hear of it being called 'lying', as a novelist has to exercise her imagination…

The bus trundled into the yard at Kalaroonta, sixty kids bent on fun, two teachers and five parents bent on keeping some sort of order. We sorted out the bunks, then went outside to explore until teatime. We were free within certain bounds, and had fun fossicking in the mullock heaps, getting filthy and finding blue azurite or green malachite, or sometimes a bit of native copper.

The teachers had organised a talk by a local that night, on the history of copper mining. Everyone else thought that was so b-o-r-i-n-g, but I was a tiny bit interested, as my dad had been appointed manager of the new mining operation. We'd probably have to come and live up here, which would be cool except I'd miss Jess. A world shortage, and therefore price rise, of copper, had led to the mines being opened up again. Jess was very interested, as she claimed to have an ancestor who had disappeared without trace during the early years of copper mining.

Anyway, we had to go to this talk, and at question time Jess put up her hand and said, 'Excuse me, sir, my great-great-great-grandfather was a copper miner here and he was the one you told us about who disappeared.'

The speaker looked a bit stunned but made the mistake of asking for more.

'He came over in the First Fleet because his mother was sentenced to seven years' transportation, and as he was only a boy of fourteen without a father, he had to come too. He was a good-looking lad and the captain picked him out from all the convicts to be his cabin boy.'

Nerdy Nigel wore a look of extreme disbelief, but the others seemed to swallow it.

She went on, 'He found all sorts of work after they arrived, farms, factories, cleaning, deckhand… Eventually he left his mother and got work on the railway, travelling to Adelaide and then up here to Kalaroonta. He got married and worked in the mines. One day he never came back from work. His wife looked for him, cried for him, the whole town did all they could, but he was never found. He had three children by this time. One of them of course was my great-great-grandfather.'

'Really?' said the speaker. 'That's all very interesting, young lady.' He couldn't call her a liar in front of her classmates, but Nigel would deal with her later.

Over supper Nigel said, 'Well, that caps all your creative anachronisms so far, Jess. If you're going to be a historical novelist, you'd better start getting your research in order.'

'What do you mean?' She and Nigel were the only ones in the class to know what anachronisms were, but she wanted to know what he meant by the remark.

'Well, the last time you told that story, he'd come as a sea captain, no sign of a convict mother, and settled in Sydney, raised a family, and it was his grandson who came over here. Caught a ship from Botany Bay en route to Perth, got caught in horrendous weather in the bight, came up Spencer Gulf for a bit of shelter and kept going, curious to know what was up here, and how far the gulf extended. For a start, if he came as a convict with the First Fleet, who had built the factories?

And what about the railway and trains to Adelaide and up here? Get real! And remember, South Australia didn't have convicts!'

She and Nigel liked each other in an intellectual kind of way, but she hated him with a passion when he found her out. Pointing out her anomalies, he called it, said he was doing her a favour. She went purple and hurried off to bed.

Next day Mrs Prescott had organised an orienteering course. That was how she taught mapping, and we'd done the basics in the school yard. We had to find our way around a set course, using only a map and compass and being timed. Jess and I went off together, talking more than concentrating and running. At one control point, Jess decided to remove her jumper, simultaneously ripping off her hearing aid and sending it flying down into a gully. In a flash she was down there after it, before she lost sight of it, but being Jess, lost her footing and slid much further than she intended. She was scrambling back up when she found the boot.

'Cass, look here.' she yelled. 'Help me up, quick!'

(My name is Cassandra Massey, so they call me Sassie Cassie Massey. Parents can be so thoughtless.)

The hearing aid forgotten, she scrambled to the top, complete with boot. 'It's got some moss and twigs in it, looks like a bird's nest.'

I was rolling my eyes by this time, thinking 'So what?'

She ripped out the bird's nest then screamed and dropped the boot. 'Oh, Cassie, look! Just look!' she yelled.

A crumbled human foot lay mixed with soil inside the boot, a left work boot.

'Oh, Jess… Who do you think… I know what you're thinking! Come on, we've got to take it to the police station.'

'No rush,' answered the logical, calmer Jess. 'He's been there a hundred years.'

The officer hummed and hahed and took our particulars. 'We'll have to get forensics onto this!'

Surprise surprise. But we knew there would be no DNA identification without a match. All we needed now, to find out if it was Jess's ancestor, was the rest of his identified body! The officer did let us take a photo of our find before plastic-bagging it and locking it away. Back at camp, our mates were furious they hadn't given them a look first. And we got a DNF (Did Not Finish, the ultimate shame) for our orienteering.

A historical walk was scheduled for next day, involving trudging round the town looking at old cottages, churches and a school. In one cottage Jess felt she was being hugged by an unseen presence. She stood among all the memorabilia of the family who had lived here, beds and kettles, clothes, ornaments, pictures… She looked out the same back door, at the same view as…her great-great-grandmother?…awaiting the return of her husband. Adolescent imagination, or a certain realisation that here were the spirits of her ancestors?

Jess was quiet as we moved on, and she didn't want any tea that night. Mrs Prescott had threatened certain death to anyone who teased her. We could wait!

The new mine started up, a thriving new town was built, and the boot stayed in police custody.

*

Only last week, fifteen years after our camp, a skeleton was discovered in a cave on the beach near Kalaroonta – minus the left foot.

Jess and I had lost touch when we went to uni. I was doing forensic science and she, of course, an arts degree, specialising in creative writing. I'd got married and moved away, but the small item in the paper flashed out at me and I just knew the skeleton was our man. Jess was still single and I tracked her down in Adelaide.

'Cassie! What brings this on? Haven't heard from you in yonks!' she screamed.

I read the news clip to her. 'It simply has to be our man, Jess,' I said.

I agreed to call the Kalaroonta police station, and give ourselves up as the original finders of The Boot. Now they could do a DNA match.

They did. The body and the foot belonged to a recorded criminal, missing for only forty years. Jess's schoolgirl yarn exposed, one mystery solved, but a hornet's nest of questions opened up.

Golden Wedding

Brett Davis was glum as he surveyed the books of The Vine Leaves resort where he was manager. They would have to think of some new ventures to pull in clients. They had a pool and gym, a spa in every room, a pokies room, cheap takeaway booze, a great restaurant, Sunday lunches by the lake and many activities and attractions round about, but still in winter people did not come.

'Chantelle.' He addressed his receptionist. 'How many have we booked for the Bubbly Special on Friday?' The Bubbly Special was aimed at couples – bottle of champagne in the fridge, bottle of bubble bath for the spa, dinner, bed and breakfast at a special rate.

'Just two couples, Brett. Why?'

'Well, look here. We just have to think of something else or we'll go broke.' He gave her a peck on the cheek by way of inspiration and showed her the books.

'Some places do weekend courses. We could have swimming, aerobics, maybe cooking. We've got the facilities.'

'Chantelle, you're a genius. Marvellous idea! How long will it take you to get it together?'

She should have known. She came up with the ideas and, for every idea he accepted, guess who got to do the work?

A month later they held their first cooking class, for unattached blokes who could only manage beans on toast or fish fingers.

'Sure, some blokes are brilliant cooks,' Chantelle had said, 'but the rest are intimidated by women in the kitchen. It has to be men-only. We'll call it 'Just add water'. Not that you do just add water but that'll make them think it's easy. You watch!'

A dozen men had booked, bachelors, single dads, widowed pensioners.

*

Frank and Julie Maidment had been married fifty years and had come to The Vine Leaves to celebrate with the Bubbly Special. After a superlative dinner (soup, salmon, sweet, cheese, bubbly and chocs), they had retired early, then made love as passionately as seventy-somethings can. Frank, satisfied with his performance and aided by his impaired hearing, lay back snoring until dawn. Julie lay awake for two hours, hearing every word on the television in room 107, along with loud conversation, running water, banging doors and grunts and groans.

In desperation at eleven-fifty, she rang down.

'Good evening. Reception, Brett speaking.'

'Julie Maidment here, room 108. Brett, it's not evening. In ten minutes it will be tomorrow and the racket next door is making sleep impossible. Can you do something?'

She heard Brett's footsteps, followed by a loud knock on door 107… a second knock accompanied by calling out…a third hammering, with 'Excuse me, sir, I really do need to speak to you, please answer the door!'

A naked man opened up, hiding all but head and shoulders behind the door, glaring at the intruder. 'What the bloody hell's going on?'

'Sir, there have been complaints about the noise. Please turn down the TV and talk more quietly. It's midnight and you are disturbing people's sleep.'

'No, I bloody well will not. This is a motel and I've paid good money to come here for some privacy with my partner. Why do you think the TV is turned up loud?'

Brett retreated in embarrassed confusion, and Mr 107 returned to bed, cursing, slamming the door and turning off the TV on his way. It was over now.

As usual on holiday, Julie went for her early-morning swim at seven a.m., leaving Frank in bed with the morning paper. She let herself into the pool with her room key and slid into the welcoming warm water.

She'd swum just five laps, the last underwater, when as she surfaced she felt firm pressure on her head. A man in bathers was crouched by the deep end of the pool, glaring down at her with his huge meaty paw gripping her. She screamed and reached up to pull him away, impotently, as he simply grabbed her wrists with his other hand.

'You, I believe, are Her Ladyship from Room 108? You reported us to reception last night. Funnily enough, I don't like to be disturbed when I'm making love, but an old crone like you wouldn't understand that, I suppose. Why do you think the telly was turned up, you silly cow? Well, I'll tell you something. You won't be swimming any more. You won't be drying off and climbing into warm dry clothes and going in to breakfast. Forget bacon and eggs, this is *it* for you.'

Julie's screams reverberated around the tiled, glassed-in pool as she struggled, trying to scratch and bite Mr 107. He had to shut her up. He yanked her by the hair, took her chin in a pistol grip as though he were going to give her mouth to mouth, then plunged her head beneath the surface. He smiled to himself. He'd passed by the restaurant where the cooking classes were to be held, and seen the notice, 'Just Add Water. Men Only.' I'll just add water to her, and there'll be a hatful of blokes to take the blame, he thought.

Julie gulped, inhaled lungfuls of chlorinated water, struggled but soon went limp. Mr 107 left.

*

Frank kept checking his watch. If Julie were much longer, they'd miss breakfast. At last he put down his paper and headed to the pool to investigate. She'd taken the only room key to gain access, but he could look through the steamy windows. All he could see was something floating in the pool... Realisation dawned; he gasped, breathing Julie's name as he passed out.

A small squad of cooking hopefuls, planning on a quick swim before class, found him. Jack Forster ran to the office to report, while Marty

Jones, fresh from a first aid course, started work on bringing Frank round. No one thought to look into the pool room.

Brett was going off duty, but grumpily managed to phone for an ambulance and wait for its arrival. Couldn't have the old geezer carking it with a heart attack on his premises.

Three of the remaining cooks meanwhile had entered the pool room. What confronted them only happened in fiction.

'Oh my God, it's the old lady, here to celebrate her golden wedding.' Barry Wilson took charge, sending Matt Smith to the poor beleaguered Brett in the office to get the police and another ambulance, while he and Andy Jervis worked on the victim. They dragged Julie out of the water, turned her over and tried to drain her lungs before beginning CPR, but Julie was very, very dead.

Mercifully the police arrived, complete with forensic pathologist, and took over. They had frozen the building, not allowing anyone to leave. Mr 107 was in his room, showering off Julie's DNA, dressing and mentally perfecting his story. His partner wondered what made him so snappy this morning, hoping they'd try to reignite last night's lovemaking now he was back from the pool.

The cooking instructor arrived, and his remaining students heard the news as they rolled up, every one a suspect. Instead of cooking, they got a grilling, one by one, as to their whereabouts. It had been established that Julie had been dead only a few minutes, and each could vouch for the other. Except for the would-be swimmers, they were every one in their rooms until breakfast.

A room key was needed to access the pool, pretty much ruling out an intruder, as there was no sign of breaking and entering. The movements of the other elderly couple were nil, as they were still in bed, unaware of the commotion. Brett had a watertight alibi confirmed by Chantelle. That left the occupants of Room 107 still to be accounted for.

The police began their routine. Full name, age, address…

'Michael Darren Chapman,' lied Mr 107. 'Look, I was just here for a night with my partner, if you must know. I never went anywhere near the bloody pool. You can ask Kerry. If my wife finds out about this, my marriage, my family and my business will be ruined. I'll be a laughing stock.

'If you are innocent, sir, you have nothing to fear. If guilty, well, too bad, I'm afraid, you'll be in jail anyway.'

Kerry, in no mood for love, was waiting in the interview queue wondering why Mr 107 had been so snappy this morning, and why the interview was taking so long. Had he been framed or was he a murderer?

A constable came in from the pool and spoke privately to the officer dealing with 'Chapman'. Bruising on Julie's head and neck indicated what had happened. Despite the whole thing happening more or less under water, DNA tests were being conducted on Julie's hair and scalp, and samples would be taken from everyone in the building. They complied readily enough, wanting their innocence established. Having given their particulars, all were released but told not to leave the state, pending the DNA results.

Despite her dunking in chlorinated water, DNA from five different people was found on Julie: Frank of course, Barry Wilson, Andy Jervis, Mr 107…and his partner Kerry. Frank was of course immediately eliminated from enquiries. Circumstantial evidence indicated number one suspect was Mr 107. Barry and Andy had only each other's word by way of evidence, Mr 107 and Kerry ditto. Supposing the perpetrator had worn gloves, leaving no direct body contact?

The pressure of the murderer's fingers on Julie's scalp had left barely perceptible fingerprints in her natural oils, which matched Mr 107's, and bruises the size of his finger ends.

The cooking classes were a huge success, scores of men wanting to learn how to 'Just add water', helped along of course by the venue being a murder scene. Brett's books had never looked better, but poor Frank would never forget his golden wedding.

Unreal Estate

Darren Mercer was a brash, arrogant thirty-year-old who gloried in his friends calling him Merciless Mercer. During a boozy weekend at Mercer Hall (no connection with any relatives), he bragged that he intended to buy a house like that and 'breed till I fill it up'. Drunk as he was at the time, the idea grew on him. Yes, that was exactly what he would do. He was good-looking, a man of the world oozing *savoir faire*. Who wouldn't marry him if he also had a big house?

Back in his rented flat, he scanned the real estate in the papers and on the internet. Sober now, he began to realise the difficulties of achieving his boast. He would need the money his mates thought he had. He mentally discarded everything as too small or too expensive, and opted to visit an agent, one Randolph Pipirelli.

Pipirelli, all smarm and grease, strode out to meet the driver of the shiny new Mercedes, borrowed from one of Darren's spoilt-rich-boy friends. Darren had created the desired effect with the car and was dressed to match.

'Good morning, sir. How may we help you?'

As expected, this pseudo-toff was seeking something very special.

'Are there any large houses hereabouts? Everywhere I look they're just too small. I'm happy to go to the country but I must have rooms, rooms, rooms, lofty ceilings, several bathrooms, at least two storeys, and extensive grounds. And no neighbours. I need space! Space for my horses, dogs, large family and army of friends.'

'We do have a place answering that description, but it's in a very dilapidated state, that's why we haven't put it on the Net. Restoring it in the manner it deserves will cost megabucks. I can take you out to see it, but…'

Darren didn't hesitate. Keeping face with his entourage was all-important and there weren't too many mansions around.

Pipirelli smelled money. 'It comes up for auction next week, sir. Not many people have seen it because of its location and state of disrepair. It's called Rockville Manor, on five hundred hectares at Rockleigh. The owners believe it's jinxed, as no daughters have been born to the family for three generations, and all the sons are handicapped in some way. Between you and me, sir, I think it's drugs.'

Darren's skin prickled. He'd dabbled a little in marijuana, but mostly it was booze, fags and pokies that took his money. But if this mob were forced to sell because of a drug problem… He entertained the thought that he could, let's say, *acquire* some drugs from this dysfunctional family and sell them on.

He forced his mind back to inconsequential chat with Pipirelli during the hour's drive to Rockville Manor.

The house was not visible from the road, being down a long, winding, tree-lined driveway. They drove past a dry dam, observing broken-down fences, rusting machinery and fallen trees. The house brooded silently on the edge of a small copse, which darkened it still further.

The two men climbed the crumbling front steps, Pipirelli unlocking a heavy timber door with an old-fashioned key that wouldn't have debarred any serious intruder. The porch was littered with broken tiles. They found rat holes in the wooden skirtings, cobwebs festooning the ceiling, and a nest of bees. Some windows were boarded up, the cellar door jammed, paint peeling. Telltale surviving plants in the garden told of its being much loved in a long-gone past. However, there were many large rooms, the structure was basically sound and the outbuildings befitted a man of means. Darren wanted Rockville Manor; Pipirelli was anxious.

'How long since it was inhabited?'

'About thirty years. The last generation refused to live here. Too big, too costly to maintain, too far from the city, then there's the jinx. They just let it go, but they had a marijuana plantation and drug lab until a bushwalker discovered them. The two brothers are in jail.'

Terrific, thought Darren. He'd put out feelers with the agent, attend the auction and worry about money later. 'What kind of money are they expecting?' he ventured. 'It's in a hell of a state and a long way from the city.'

'But look at the potential and the acreage! You could run a tourism venture here, a riding school, convention centre, holiday accommodation, that sort of thing. Have you ever been to Mercer Hall?'

This is where we came in, thought Darren. 'So how much?'

But of course Pipirelli was fencing. He'd have to keep the price up. He'd invent a reserve price and have a few incognito accomplices putting in false bids. Easy!

*

Darren arrived early at the auction. Five wrinkled old men were sitting, wrapped in blankets, in five wrinkled old wicker chairs on the front veranda. Darren correctly guessed them to be the remnants of the family from two generations ago. Younger family members were absent. Very few people were there, just some nosey locals with no intention of bidding. The auctioneer banged his gavel, cleared his throat and began talking up the property. When he asked for an opening bid above half a million, hands were raised, almost imperceptible nods came from somewhere in the thin crowd. When the bids reached a million, Darren slunk away, his dream destroyed, his boast blown away. Out of character for him, he had kept his mouth shut; nobody he knew was aware he was there.

So, what now? Back to the drawing board, as the cliché goes? Drugs. Rob a bank. Chat up a rich old lady. Where else do crims get their loot? Our brash know-all was so naïve.

Rockville Manor was passed in at auction. Struth, whatever was the reserve price? He had suspected rigging but…

*

Masima Tanaka was perched on a bar stool, smoking, fingering a drink, her revealing skirt above her knee, a stereotypical pick-up. It was never long before her diminutive form and glossy black hair attracted someone keen to buy her a drink. Tonight that someone was Merciless Mercer, who could spot his prize at a thousand paces. He chose a pick-up line from his portfolio; she laughed, a good sign. He asked what she was drinking, and repeated it with an extra shot. They talked. She was accompanying her businessman father as his secretary, but was bored and lonely. And rich, presumed Darren. I'll show you our city by night, then we'll go to my place for some fun. He would not take her to his scruffy rented flat, but to the tenth-floor beachfront apartment of one of his slick cronies. He imagined the conversation between them, once he had her on the couch. This was his city pad, but he had a mansion in the country. Because of the drought, times had been hard and he needed money for renovations and upgrading the racing stables. He wanted children, but couldn't ask anyone to marry him until the mansion was fit for his bride. A tenth-floor apartment was no place to rear children.

Masima had been raised in a similar place, minus the beach front. She would tell him she wanted children too, to grow up in space and freedom in Australia. He would tell her of the jinx bestowed on his mansion by the previous owners. Would it matter if they could not have daughters, pretty little Japanese girls? She would laugh, declare she wanted boys, and anyway it was the father, not the building where they were conceived, that determined the sex of the infant. Daddy had been urging her, his only child, to marry, as he wanted grandsons to inherit his empire. An old-school patriarch, he did not believe in leaving the dynasty to a mere daughter, cunning and brilliant business partner though she was.

The night went fairly well to plan. Masima was mind-blowing in bed, but when she announced her engagement to an Australian horse-breeder to Daddy, he wasn't quite dim enough to fit into slick-boy's scheme. He wanted to meet Darren, see the mansion, see the deeds, talk business before approving. Panic-stricken, Darren plotted to take Masima and Daddy to Mercer Hall, but was defeated by the problem of deeds and ownership.

Enter Pipirelli, still smelling money from Rockville Manor. Every man has his price. Every man has his PC. With a quick photocopy and cut 'n' paste job, he could falsify the Rockville Manor deeds, make them look like Mercer Hall's. He would meet them with the 'deeds' and all would be well.

Darren swaggered around, buying afternoon tea for one and all from the café on the terrace. Mercer Hall was sufficiently well appointed to impress Masima and Daddy, sufficiently in need of renovations in certain quarters for them to appreciate the need for an injection of funds. Daddy phoned Japan to report the engagement of his daughter to an Australian millionaire with huge assets but no cash flow, the deal sealed by his investment in Darren's large horse racing enterprise. They would be returning to Japan to celebrate, but meeting the suitor would have to be postponed as he was currently tied up with crucial business engagements.

Big ideas, bigger mouth, biggest mess! Damn it, Darren didn't even know this girl! Oh well, she was good in bed, he had the money now, he could divorce her later. He organised a repeat auction via a deal with one nervous Pipirelli, who couldn't shout, 'Going, going, gone to Mr Darren Mercer' fast enough. Previous aspirants were absent, put off by the first auction. The old men wanted rid of Rockville Manor. They just needed enough to set up their grandsons when they were released from prison, and had dropped the reserve. The house was his for $800,000, plus Pipirelli's considerable fee.

But this large millstone, plus an extravagant wife-to-be, needed upkeep. Could he renovate the property on borrowed money? Could he disappear? He could be 'away on business' when Masima and Daddy returned. How would he explain that they were going to live at Rockville Manor, not Mercer Hall?

Darren had studied the modus operandi of a local arsonist. The newspapers had seen fit to describe exactly how she had set numerous fires. Picking up another woman and inviting her, as his cover, for a weekend in a Mercedes, with Mercer, at Mercer, was easy. Claire was pretty and otherwise intelligent, but gullible with regard to men and their promises. He packed his incendiary devices in the boot of the Merc, stacked their cases on top, and drove off for a flaming good weekend. The first night was a ripper, spent building Claire's trust and enjoying her considerable talents in the bedroom. Next day split his mind apart, plotting to raze the building – with her inside. She didn't deserve to die but he couldn't explain her to Masima.

They were in the bar when he worked the I-gotta-go-to-the-gents trick. They retired 'for an early night' with great anticipation, after their last effort. A device was set for three-thirty a.m. He'd caress Claire to sleep, then be out of there. When Masima returned three days later, he'd take her, distraught, to see the ashes of their future home, then to see the replacement he'd bought at Rockleigh. He'd tell her the insurance money would furnish her heart's desire. They would live happily until they tired of each other, and produce several children, including girls.

But Merciless Mercer hadn't bargained for his stamina letting him down. His last romp soon plunged him into deep sleep. You could have dropped a bomb under him. Technology – or human error? – often lets us down at the crucial moment. At twenty-three-thirty precisely, the device detonated. Fire alarms screamed as the conflagration ripped through Mercer Hall. Claire awoke, yanking the comatose, naked Darren from the bed and shoving him towards the staircase. She slid down the banister towards relative safety, Darren crashed through fire-ravaged stairs into the burning morass below. Dental records and DNA tests on the remains of his burnt body left him exposed.

Masima returned to discover her lucky escape, Daddy to discover the subterfuge. The old men laughed, but Rockville Manor awaited another saviour.

The Eternal Conundrum

Roddy Dawson was the epitome of twenty-year-old university student: long hair, beard, studs and rings in almost every orifice and protrusion, perennially broke. His widowed mother allowed him to live at home free of charge in exchange for man-of-the-house jobs; this and his trusty pushbike enabled him always to have enough loot for an evening beer with the lads, and a girlfriend or three. This cosy arrangement was headed for changes he could not foresee.

'I won't be in when you come home for tea, love. I've got a doctor's appointment,' his mum told him as he donned his helmet one morning.

He thought nothing of it; she went about every couple of months for this test or that prescription, and she seemed pretty OK.

He was doing a maths/science double major, and today he was in for a lecture on intelligent design. They'd already had a forum, a debate between two Evolutionists and two Creationists (which must have been staged and sanitised, as they didn't murder each other in righteous indignation). He'd had enough of all that; years of sitting through Sunday school, followed by church and confirmation class, finally digging his heels in at age fifteen and declaring that we live in a country of religious freedom, which meant his mother could not make him go.

One would think, having lost his Dad fifteen years ago, she would be very anti-religious; what kind of god would widow a mother of three small children? Strangely, she clung to her beliefs more than ever, and was heartbroken that Roddy would have none of it. They'd had this discussion one day, along the lines of 'Only God can make a tree'…or an elephant, or an eye, and so forth.

Roddy scornfully replied 'Yeah, yeah, 'The tall trees in the greenwood, the pleasant summer sun' and all that. Mum, if there's anything you can't explain, you put it all down to God. So does this loving God make earthquakes and war, famine and disease? Does he make harmful illegal drugs or just good ones? Those kind of explanations don't cut the mustard for me any more.'

He was eating alone when his mum came home, looking already like death itself.

'Roddy…sit down, love. I've got something to tell you.'

'Oh my God (whoops, must stop saying that because there isn't one – and if there were, it would be blasphemy),' he thought, 'she's got something terrible.'

'It's…it's… Oh Roddy…' she stammered, collapsing in tears.

Roddy moved to her chair and embraced her, letting her weep. When she had quietened, he gently asked her to try again.

'It's…breast cancer, love, and I've got secondaries. It's gotten into my lymph glands, so now it will get everywhere. Doctor can't say how long, depends how the chemo and radiation and drugs go. Oh Roddy…' she sobbed, and then, 'I don't mind for myself, I mean, why *not* me, but… it's you kids, and Aunty Marlene, and all my friends…'

Roddy digested this information in stunned silence. He didn't play soccer next day. It was a semi-final but he couldn't leave his mum. Later, when she had come to terms with the situation, but not yet. He called the team manager, who gave him a serve about courage and loyalty and the importance of the game. Roddy angrily retorted that there were plenty more players but he had only one mother, and that not for much longer. They lost, to add guilt to his mix of emotions.

It turned out, however, that the captain, Jon Barton, whom they all regarded as God in boots, had half-heartedly played the worst game of his life, even managing an own goal. Roddy couldn't believe it was because of his own absence that things went pear-shaped. He knew Jon had recently split with his girlfriend, Dianna. They'd been dithering about marriage for ages, but found their religious differences irreconcilable, although Roddy didn't know who was on which side of the fence. He just dismissed it, thinking, 'Bloody religion again. Has a lot to answer for!' The girl had found a new beau, and as Jon put it, 'Older than me, heaps more dough, no contest.' The weekend before the big match, she'd gone away with this fellow and they'd taken a hot-air balloon ride. The pilot, very experienced and apparently fit, had suffered a heart attack, so the post-mortem found. No one on board had a clue how to bring the balloon down safely. It pitched and tossed in the sky for several minutes before crashing in trees on a mountainside, ripping the canopy to shreds. The pilot and five of the eight passengers died. One of them was Dianna. All week Jon'd tortured himself, decided against attending the funeral, and played soccer instead, justifying that to himself with 'Can't bring her back, the game will do me good, after all she was my ex, the team need me, it's a big match…'

Some weeks later, cycling through the suburbs on the way to uni, Roddy saw ahead of him an electrician's van almost reversed into the roadway, a man in blue overalls standing beside it, looking totally shell-shocked. Lying on the ground was a small boy of about ten, his torso partially pinned under the back wheel. Apparently his mother had sent him after his dad with Dad's lunch, left on the kitchen bench in his haste to leave for work. He was backing out rather too fast, certainly not looking for his son, when tragedy struck. Roddy brought the man out of his trance and made him help lift the vehicle off the boy, before summoning ambulance and police.

The child was conscious, pale, shaking and whimpering. He told Roddy he was dying, which of course Roddy refuted with a cheeriness he was far from feeling, as the poor kid appeared to have fatal internal injuries. He asked Roddy what it was like to die, what was Heaven like? (Geez, kids think adults know everything, and here's another brainwashed one.) Roddy said he didn't know, to which the kid replied, 'But there is a God, isn't there, mister?' (Oh hell, no, there isn't but I can't tell a dying kid that.)

'Yes, son, of course there is. Don't you worry about that. Listen, here comes the ambulance. They'll look after you and fix you up like new.' His reward was a faint smile, the last the boy would give.

Roddy was beginning to have bad dreams; two people in his orbit killed within weeks, his mother looking death in the face. He was preoccupied at uni, and late with a couple of assignments.

His science tutor, Dr Adrian Maslen, was a man of great stature in the science world, professor, broadcaster, author of dozens of scientific papers and a few great tomes – and well-known for his seemingly incongruous beliefs. He called Roddy aside after one tute. 'What's eating you, Roddy?'

'Sorry?'

'Come on, don't pretend. You're an A student. In recent weeks you've been somewhere else, not with us in tutes or lectures, two late assignments with no explanation, and I overheard a couple of your mates complaining that you were…well, in their own vernacular, they said you were bad-tempered and moody. So come on, spill, what's up?'

Roddy was silent for a while, then began to relate the events quietly, before the floodgates opened. He could trust this man. When he'd done, there was a silence between them, broken by Roddy's outburst of 'You believe in God, don't you, Adrian?'

Dr Maslen, silent again, weighed up the complexities of the tortured lad before him, then, 'Yes, Roddy, I do. People say that doesn't square with my scientific background, but each person has to make up his or her own mind, including you. If you like, we'll talk about it some more when you're calmer, or I'll prepare the ground for you with a student counsellor or chaplain. Now, go have some lunch. You're due in the lab in half an hour.'

'Yes. Thanks, Adrian. Thanks for your understanding.'

Things went along quietly for a few months. Roddy passed third year, but his mother was not improving. He decided to work only part time during summer vac so he could give her more time, do more at home and take her to appointments. Midway through February, she needed home visits and was obviously sinking. The doctor wanted her in a palliative care centre but she insisted on staying at home. All they could do now was keep her out of pain until the end.

One day she asked Roddy to come and sit with her. 'Son,' she began, 'you've meant so much to me and done so much for me. It will soon be time to go. You have the capacity to achieve great things. Please,

please, continue with your studies. Remember the good times we had, remember me but don't waste good time grieving. And Roddy…' She stifled tears. 'Roddy…I hope one day you will come to believe.'

Roddy was speechless and just sat there holding her hand. She died forty-eight hours later.

Uni began again in March, Roddy's fourth year. He was eager to return, to report to Dr Maslen that he'd lost his mother, but hoped he was now back on track. Surely he would encounter no more tragedy.

But Dr Maslen was dead. A stroke on New Year's Day was at first put down to over-imbibing the night before, as he was a devoted Scot who revelled in Hogmanay, but he was misjudged. They found an inoperable, malignant brain tumour.

The bad dreams began again. First it was his mother, crying that now she knew there really was a God, and Roddy had better believe it. He woke up sweating and shaking, believing he'd heard his mother's voice, telling himself it was just the grief, it would settle down, he wasn't going mad.

But then the little boy started. He'd been a scallywag, often in trouble at school, a prankster in Sunday school, but near death had suddenly hoped he was wrong, desperately wanting Roddy to assure him there was a God and that he'd go to Heaven, whatever that was. 'Your mum was right, Roddy,' he said. (Hang on, how did the kid know his name, or what conversations he'd had with his mother?) 'God's right here and he said to tell you. There's no school, no pain, nobody gets punished and the sun shines all the time. Saw your mum yesterday and she told me all about you.'

Roddy knew how to fix the problem. Only temporarily, of course. He'd overheard a conversation in the canteen where he was able to unravel the code-speak and learn where he could get marijuana. Not difficult. Of course he would never graduate to harder stuff, this was only for temporary relief from the voices…

When Dianna, the soccer captain's ex-girlfriend, started on him, he really did question his sanity. She woke him one night, screaming that she'd been right, there was no God, no Heaven, no Hell, but she didn't know where she was now. Obviously not complete oblivion. She was talking to Roddy, wasn't she? Was this limbo? If so, the fanatical ravings of the priesthood were coming true, therefore…but…anyway, Roddy, it's all crap. You relax. Christ, thought Roddy. (Hell, maybe he's true too! I can't handle this! Must be the marijuana; it was supposed to help.)

He went to bed expecting to hear from Professor Maslen. That encounter took a while, and Roddy found himself getting interested in seances and spiritualism, almost trying to pray to Adrian like the aficionados of his church did to the saints. At last he showed up, but Roddy found he just had to listen and couldn't talk back, a new concept for him.

'Roddy,' came the voice, 'I guess you want my answer because you don't want to believe your mum was right, or that the mischievous little boy now knows it too. After all, in life he'd have pulled your leg over anything, and your mum would have said what she did because belief is more comforting when you are facing death. There are still mysteries surrounding what Dianna told you. She liked you and would have told you there's no God because that's what you wanted to think. At the same time, she'd have wanted to comfort you. So where are you now? You can't answer, you'll just have to think about it. Didn't I tell you: each person has to work it out for him or herself, including you. Goodnight, Roddy.'

Roddy felt as though his brain, his intelligent thinking self, had been put through a washing machine. After all he'd been through, he was no nearer to knowing the truth, and isn't that what scientists were, seekers after truth? Which of the spirits were lying, which telling the truth? He felt like the prisoner with the jailers, one of whom lied and one told the truth about which door led to freedom. Adrian had sat on the fence, Dianna had said the same as she did in life, so had his mum, but the boy had been pleased to say he'd been wrong. Would a little boy be able to invent that story? Roddy was back at square one, a ship without a rudder. He wasn't ready to fly solo yet on this one.

Crisis On Kosciuszko

'Mum? *Mum!*

At that moment the line went dead, as Andrew's wife Monika appeared at his office door, his briefcase in hand.

'Hi, thought I'd better… Darling, *what's wrong?*'

He reached out for her, face ashen, body shaking. 'It's…Mum and Dad…

*

Ken and Liz were keen bushwalkers taking a trip to the Snowy Mountains before the bushfire season. Ken was a key radio operator for his local CFS. brigade. It was now or not until autumn for a well-earned break. The Snowies are the perfect bushwalking location after snowmelt, quiet after the skiers have gone and before summer holiday hordes descend. They hooked up their caravan and headed for Jindabyne, securing an idyllic spot on the lakeside.

Perfect weather greeted their first morning. They left early for Charlotte Pass, planning to tackle the Main Range walk, the glorious twelve-kilometre traverse to the seven-thousand-foot summit of Mt Kosciuszko. The first challenge was to wade barefoot, knee-deep across the Snowy River, in spate with melted snow. Sharp, slippery rocks and near-freezing, rushing water made for a hazardous and painful crossing but, this accomplished, they vowed to complete the loop, returning from the summit the easy way via nine kilometres of gravel road.

'That's *it*,' declared Liz, 'I'm *not* going back through that for love or money, and certainly not for fun!'

Ken didn't argue. They dried their red and goosebumped legs, re-donned their socks and hiking boots and strode on. Three kilometres ahead they came upon a steep, icy slope, snow that had been thawed and refrozen, plummeting to a rocky gorge.

'Ken…we can't…'

Ken poked his stick into the snow, stamped around, plodded a few yards into the bank and declared it safe if they were careful. Supported by his stick, he dug his heels in and made level footprints.

Liz quipped, 'In my husband's steps I trod, where the snow lay dinted,' and inched after him – with no stick.

Success! Another two kilometres saw them at Blue Lake, an idyllic spot for morning tea and a reassessment before plugging on to Mt Caruthers, where their jaws dropped. They were confronted by a massif of frozen snow underlain by rocks, rushing streams of meltwater, large voids and spiky scrub, covering a forty-degree slope into the valley below. Ken said no way. Liz said maybe. Negotiation led to their climbing upwards along a snow-free channel through thick wet scrub, until they reached a flat plateau some distance from the track – or where they guessed the track to be, buried under snow. Slowly they edged along, repeating the King Wenceslas method, until the plateau gave way to a slope descending to the invisible track.

It happened too suddenly. They had become almost blasé about creeping along, when Ken stumbled on a hidden rock, slipped and fell headlong. There was nothing to hold on to, no protruding rock or tree, just ice, ice and more ice precipitating him down, down to certain death when he hit the rocks below.

Liz opened her mouth to scream but no sound came. She threw herself to the ground, digging her toes into his last footprints. Ken's stick had jammed against the rock when he fell, he'd dropped it, and this temporarily saved Liz. She grabbed it, dragged one foot on to the rock and dug the stick into the snow, fumbling for the mobile phone. She could move neither forward nor back, and anyway, ahead was more impassable ice, behind was the previous such slope and the rising river. She was trapped literally between the proverbial rock and hard place.

Dial 000. Teeth chattering uncontrollably, she outlined her plight. Suicidal to try to reach Ken, who was in more ways than one, beyond reach. A helicopter would come. She was to keep warm, stay still, conserve her energy, try to stay calm. Calm! My husband dead, myself likely to be if I move a muscle…

She dialled the children who lived in Australia. No answer. Answering service. Engaged. She dialled their son in Budapest. It was only seven a.m. there but Andrew would be in his office, stealing a march on the school day before the children arrived. He picked up the phone on the first ring.

'Andrew, it's Mum. I'm in a bit of a pickle. In fact…' She burst into tears.

'Mum, whatever's wrong?' and after a pause, 'Please, try to stop crying so you can tell me…'

She collected herself. 'It's Dad. We're on the Main Range track, you know, the back road up Kosciuszko. It's covered in ice and snow and… Dad slipped. I can't see him, he's over the edge.' More sobs.

Stunned silence in Budapest.

'I've dialled 000. They're sending a helicopter to get me and look for him. Son, I…just…want…to tell you…how much we love you. I don't think Dad can have survived. If I slip, I won't either. Just try and concentrate on the good times we had… You know where our wills and funeral stuff are.'

How can she be so calm, so controlled, as though she thought the whole thing out before it happened, what she would do and say, he thought.

'Mum…hang in there. I love you both too.' At that he choked up and there was silence between them until a low hum with a regular beat, beat, beat could be heard getting closer.

'Andrew, the chopper's here…stay on the line…'

Like he was going to hang up!

Liz gave thanks for her lurid orange jacket and blue pants, beacons against the snow. The chopper circled, she waved her free arm, and it came in low with a rush of air that almost dislodged her. While the pilot held it steady, her rescuer descended on a hawser with a harness. In the ensuing kerfuffle to winch Liz up into the chopper and safety, she dropped the phone, which went skidding away into oblivion.

*

In Budapest, the children were beginning to arrive. The secretary came up with a message, knocked, coughed discreetly when confronted by her boss in tears in his wife's arms, and retreated on a signal from Monika.

Monika sat Andrew down, and rang for coffee. Calmer for her presence, he knew she would know what to do. Ordinarily, so would he, but this was no ordinary situation. Not every day do one's parents go skidding off a mountainside.

'Moni, what can we *do*? My dad's lying dead at the foot of a mountain twenty thousand kilometres away and I feel so helpless!'

Holding him close, she said, 'I know, love. But what could you have done if you were there? Held his hand? Stopped him doing these things? You can't do that any more than he could do it to you. It's been a dreadful accident but…one day you'll be comforted by the knowledge that he was doing what he wanted to do. You need to ring the Australian embassy, get them to contact the emergency services in the nearest town to the mountain.'

He needed focus, something positive to do. It was better to make him do it himself. He didn't want to cut that phone line, just in case, just in case…maybe the battery was dead, maybe she'd dropped it, maybe… He gave that phone to Monika to listen, hoping against hope for contact, and picked up the other one.

Twenty interminable minutes later the embassy rang back. 'Mr Morrison? We have good news and bad. Your mother is safe, but as yet your father has not been found. Your mother dropped her mobile during the rescue, that's why you were cut off. We are so very sorry but they are doing all they can. They will continue looking, because your mother insists she does not need to go to hospital and just wants to find him. We'll keep you posted.'

Andrew collapsed into a chair as the cold, hard fact of his father's death began to sink in.

Suddenly there was a crackle from the phone that Monika was holding somewhat reluctantly after all this time.

'Hello…is anybody there?' The voice was familiar, Yorkshire tempered by a faint Australian overtone.

'*Ken!*'

Andrew leaped up in disbelief, grabbed the phone.

'*Dad!* Oh Dad, where *are* you, what happened, you're alive, oh hell, are you OK, Mum's in the chopper…'

'Steady on, lad. I just had a bit of a rollercoaster ride down the mountain, faster than Dreamworld and all for free. I went like the clappers on the ice, got jettisoned off an overhang, then landed in a snowbank on some scrubby bushes. In fact, I think I'm on top of a tree. I can't figure out why they can't find me. Hope they do before this lot melts. Seems Mum chucked her phone away, 'cos I'm holding it now, must've followed me down, reckon she got tired of talking to you…'

Carrots

They had argued over such a trivial matter. Jedd was quick-tempered and knew he was headed for anger management counselling; he soon cooled down, but usually by then the damage was done. Every time Polly breathed, he criticised, but she claimed to love him, said she'd change him.

This time it was the vegetables. She'd served carrots last night, and here they were again. First time it was with steak, roast spuds and cauliflower. Tonight it was with broccoli, mashed potatoes and pork chops. But he didn't want carrots again, no way Jose, and the gravy was cold and the chops undercooked. He picked up his plate, threw it in her face and ran out of the house. Polly, in tears, meekly cleared up the mess.

An hour passed. A cold anger crept over her. This was the last straw and she was no camel; she wouldn't have her back broken. She showered, changed, packed and checked outside. He'd left his car! She'd secretly had a key copied so, looking around fearfully, she loaded her things, put the car in neutral and released the handbrake so it would roll silently out of the driveway. Once on the road, she started the engine and fled to her mother, who took her in and agreed to take her to a women's shelter in the morning.

Jedd returned at midnight, violently drunk, his rage fuelled by beer and whisky on an empty stomach. He had rape in mind. When the wherewithal was missing, he went berserk. He smashed the TV, hurled furniture around, punched a hole in the wall then started on the kitchen. That slut hadn't even washed the dishes, smash, crash! Then he realised the car was missing.

His only wheels were on a rusty old pushbike, but that'd take him to find an unlocked car. He wobbled along, but he'd roused the neighbours, who'd ignored the earlier fracas. Fred from next door, with his son Jason, followed him at a discreet distance, carrying a stick for self-defence.

Jedd came to number 21, where Mrs James had forgotten to lock her old Holden. He'd learnt to hotwire a car when he was Jason's age. When Jason and Fred approached him, he swung a punch at Fred, who ducked as Jason wielded the stick, felling Jedd.

'Oh my God, *Jason*, what have you *done*?' They ran home, not knowing whether Jedd was dead or alive. They calmly had another beer and went back to bed. Fred's wife had not even missed them.

Sprightly Mrs James had a hairdressing appointment and bounced out of the house smiling – until she noticed her car bonnet up. When she saw Jedd, sprawled on her driveway in a pool of blood, she fainted.

The postman found her just coming round. A level-headed young man, he didn't panic. He took Mrs James inside, then returned to Jedd. No breathing. No pulse. Cold. Dead.

*

Polly collapsed at the news. If only she hadn't given him carrots again…

Double Trouble, Double Joy

Zac and Kirsty were as excited as eight-year-old twins can be when Uncle Nick suggested taking them sand-boarding on Moreton Island. He'd enlist the help of Grandma Madge and they'd catch the ferry from Manly. Unsure of facilities on the island, Madge had packed everything, as grandmas do. Grandpa said he got seasick on a wet lawn, so Uncle Rusty was taking him and their dad golfing for the day.

'Better than chewing your nails at home, Steve,' said Grandpa. 'Baby'll come when it's ready, and you've got your mobile.'

Dolphins greeted the boat, swimming alongside and showing off as they chugged across Moreton Bay. Zac asked if they could feed them when they got there. They arrived just as the sand-boarding kiosk was opening.

'Here, you two. Slip, slop, slap,' reminded Madge, as Nick paid and they lined up for their boards.

For the first run, Madge would take Kirsty, Nick would take Zac, then they would be on their own. The children didn't seem to notice the steep climb up the dune. It was a race to see who could do the most runs, but Uncle Nick was hampered by a sprained ankle gained at rugby practice. Grandma was just plain hampered, but having a go anyway.

It was on about her tenth trip that Kirsty lost control of her board, and spun away into a swale. Once over the shock, she dissolved into giggles, looked around to show off to Zac and started scrambling back. When a couple of heads suddenly appeared over the crest of the next dune ,she skidded to a halt, the colour draining from her face as a naked man appeared. His companion disappeared from sight, to dress hastily in embarrassed confusion.

The man strode towards Kirsty, yelling, 'What do you want, kid? Just clear off and mind your own business,' interspersed with rude words.

Giggles turned to silence, to racking sobs as fear engulfed her, then screams of terror as he picked her up and shook her violently.

'Where's Kirsty?' asked Zac, with that sixth sense twins have.

All three looked around. Yes, where was Kirsty?

They struggled off over the dunes. Nick, forgetting the sprained ankle, strode ahead until he saw previously obscured figures two hundred metres away, then stopped in horror as he saw Kirsty's plight. Zac set off to run to Kirsty, but Grandma Madge grabbed him in time. Nick pushed his mobile phone into Madge's hands and told her to call for help, as he had no idea how this would turn out. He knew coverage was as patchy as his mother's capability with technology, but pinned his hopes on her getting through. He ran towards Kirsty as fast as he could, despite the ankle. His first instinct was to pulverise the man, but he'd heard too much of both aggressor and retaliator going to jail in such a situation. He slowed down as he approached the pair, to catch his breath and think. There was a second person cowering in the dunes. So the man had reinforcements, a female judo black belt for all he knew.

'Excuse me, is there a problem? Please put her down.'

Confused and disarmed by Nick's politeness, the enraged man dropped Kirsty like a naughty kitten. She ran to Nick and hid behind him.

'Nosey brat. You'd think we could have some privacy here.'

Don't inflame him further, Nick. Kirsty is safe, walk away, walk away.

'I'm sorry, sir. She's just a little girl who lost control of her sand-board.'

Madge and Zac had arrived. Madge scooped Kirsty up and hugged her. They all walked away together.

Time for some cure-all, ice cream. They returned their boards and walked slowly towards the kiosk, completely forgetting that Grandma Madge had sent for the police. Kirsty asked if the man had been skinny-dipping.

'Probably,' he said, 'and sunbaking, when you landed on their patch.'

She giggled. 'I hope he got his bum sunburned.'

That's our girl, bouncing back already.

There was some time yet before the boat was to return, so Nick suggested a swim. Oh yes, Zac, and the dolphins. And their picnic.

'Swimming' meant jumping into the waves, body surfing, splashing, giggling and trying to dunk Uncle Nick. The children needed some cheering up; in fact, they all did. Exhausted at last, they walked up the beach to find their clothes.

Madge suddenly clutched her chest, gasped, 'Nick I don't feel so...' and collapsed on the sand.

Nick reached for his mobile, then remembered his mother had it to call the police. The police! Well, they'll have to wait, we have bigger fish to fry. Looking around, they discovered they were a good hundred metres further along the beach than the place where they'd entered the water, unwittingly carried along by the longshore drift. Handbag and clothes were already being licked by the incoming tide.

Nick recovered his phone from Madge's bag but they seemed to be in a blind spot for reception. Think, Nick, think. He looked around, realising that he had seen no sign of the lifeguards. It would be very difficult to have them out here. What was that at the first aid class? DR ABCD. Danger. Get her further up the beach. Response. No response. Airway. Clear. Breathing. Very shallow and intermittent. Circulation. A faint pulse but was he doing it right? Defibrilator – fat chance out here. Oh gosh, this was his mother, probably dying right there in front of him. Should he start expired-air resuscitation? He thought he'd understood at the class, but now it was real and urgent...

'Kirsty, Zac, listen.' He squatted to their level. 'Grandma is in trouble. Run as fast as you can and stop the first people you meet and ask them to call an ambulance.'

Kirsty looked troubled, unwilling to leave Nick and Grandma, or approach strangers, after her ordeal.

Zac yanked her by the arm with a 'Come *on*, Kirsty, Grandma could be dying!'

They ran down the beach, leaving Nick to do his best. They met a middle-aged couple and gasped out their story.

The woman acted swiftly. 'Brian, phone the ambulance station and take care of these two,' then, explaining that she was a doctor, set off at a run towards Madge and Nick. 'I can't do much more without my medical bag,' she gasped to Nick. 'It's in the car on the mainland, injections, defib machine, the works, but there's an ambulance station here and they're marvellous.' She got to work, breathing into Madge, monitoring her pulse.

Nick relaxed somewhat; at least she would know if she should start full-blown CPR.

Time was critical – seconds count, every minute seemed like an hour – but he heard the siren after only four minutes. The ambos worked on Madge even as they were moving her. Plans were already in place to helicopter her to Brisbane.

Nick and Dr Spinks walked back along the beach to find Mr Spinks and the children. Mr Spinks had held up the boat, due to leave fifteen minutes ago.

Nick tried to comfort and reassure the children, with a confidence he did not feel and which the children could see right through.

'She's your mum, isn't she, Uncle Nick?'

'Yes, Zac, she's my mum,' and, deflecting the conversation, 'I wonder how your mum is getting on?'

They had forgotten, amid the traumas of the day, about their mum.

They arrived home to a note from dad: 'Baby coming, gone to hospital.'

They were all beyond exhaustion. Grandpa had made them some tea but they pecked at it listlessly. Uncle Rusty and Grandpa went off to Madge's hospital, while Nick gently coaxed the children off to the shower and bed.

About eight o'clock the phone rang. It was their dad.

'Hi, Nick. How was your day? Are Mum and Dad there? We've got news!'

Nick decided Steve had enough on his mind without hearing of their traumatic day. 'Well, actually…' he began, then choked up.

'Nick, what's up? Put Mum and Dad on.'

Nick thought he could hear a baby crying. He took the phone to Kirsty's room, and woke Zac.

'Hey, listen, you two, what can you hear?'

Their faces lit up. 'A baby, a baby. Is it ours? Is it a boy or a girl?'

An exhausted mum, Sharon, came on the line. 'Hi, you two. Did you have a good day?'

Silence.

Nick took the phone. 'We've had quite an adventure, but…do I have another niece or nephew?'

'Well, are you sitting comfortably? Both!'

'Both what? Oh you mean…both a boy and a girl? *Sharon*, how could you not know it was twins again?'

Zac and Kirsty grinned at each other. He'd wanted a boy, she a girl. Zac would call his baby brother Jack, "cos it rhymes with me and it sounds cool.' Kirsty would call her baby sister Olivia "cos it's a lovely name and I don't want the same initials.' They forgot for a while the traumas of the day, amid this new excitement.

Nick eventually took the phone. Steve would have to know about his mum, the rest would wait.

*

Madge lay in her hospital bed on a drip and a monitor, wondering why she was there but becoming gradually aware. She remembered the trouble in the dunes, and swimming with the children, then…nothing until now. Steve came into the ward with flowers and a photo of the babies with Sharon. This was her first inkling that she was again the grandmother of twins, and the news lit up every cell of her fragile body.

Steve knew now about Kirsty's ordeal but didn't discuss it. After a brief visit he sought out a doctor for a prognosis.

'Well, Mr Metcalf, we think she will eventually be fine, but it will take a long time. It was a very severe heart attack, and only through the cooperation of all concerned in getting her here quickly has she survived. She'll be here a while, and she's scheduled for a quadruple bypass later. Anyway, I understand congratulations are in order for you? Just what your mum needs to help her get better.'

While Steve was at the hospital, another mobile call came in. Nick took it.

'Mr Metcalf? Manly police. You called us out today on Moreton Island. Some fracas with another person. Was this by any chance a hoax, sir?'

'A hoax?' said Nick, incredulous, 'My eight-year-old niece attacked by a naked man, a hoax?'

'Now look, sir, we turned out and searched the area and found no one. Perhaps you could explain? Wasting police time is a very serious offence, you know.'

Nick blurted out the facts in a torrent, and added, 'And before you ask, no, I can't prove it unless you'll take the word of the children.'

'What about your mother?'

'She's in hospital. She had a severe heart attack after the incident.'

That quietened the officer somewhat, but he rang off with 'We'll be in touch.'

*

Nick took the children to see Grandma Madge next day.

She was much brighter, greeting him with 'Look, Nick, I've got something to show you.' Out came her digital camera, miraculously unaffected by its dunking in the sea. She displayed with some pride a shot of the man shaking Kirsty. His mum was not such a stranger to modern technology after all.

'Oh, Mum, you've got me out of strife again, probably not for the last time!'

Crossroads

Felicity Randell was glad to marry Mitchell Ross. In fact, she would have been glad to marry almost anyone in order to change her name. She did not consider 'Randy' a fitting moniker for an RN, a respectable young professional woman, and 'Flick' was almost as bad.

For several years it was all wine and roses with Mitchell: nice house, two adorable children, satisfying careers… Mitchell was a rising star in the police force, a detective going for his final DI exams. So Felicity was stunned beyond belief when he came home one day and turned away from her usual welcoming embrace. She found herself staring at his back as he announced, 'It's over, Felicity.' Felicity: what he called her when he was seriously upset or angry.

Apopleptic, she stammered, 'W-what do you mean?'

'Us,' he said. 'You and me. I can't take any more.'

'*Mitchell!*' she yelled hysterically. 'Have you lost it totally? I know things have been hard for you, losing your dad and swotting for exams, and all the trouble with Paula, but…I've tried to support you, take the pressure off. What am I supposed to have done?'

He stood, impassive, for aeons lasting about thirty seconds, then exploded. 'You've supported me? Look at the mess around here – no clean shirt for tomorrow, dinner not even started – and who watches the kids' sport at weekends while you're out gallivanting with your mother? Eh, who? When did you last see a game?'

'Mum needs my support. You're just under too much stress at the moment and…'

'Too right I am, and what are you doing about it? No, Flick, it's over. You can have the house, the kids can live with you, I just want out and that's my last word.'

A huge wave of silence built up between them, broken when Mitchell strode to their room and started shoving clothes into a suitcase.

Felicity followed him. 'Mitchell, I didn't know, you never said… I'm so sorry, does it have to be like this? What about the kids…?'

Oh, she must have been blind, deaf and stupid, she thought. What would she tell Matthew and Jade? They'd just lost their grandpa after a protracted battle with cancer, and now their dad was walking out. How would they cope? She threw herself onto the bed and sobbed.

'No use bawling, it's too late, I'm outa here for good,' Mitchell raged as he left.

Matthew and Jade heard the commotion and came from their rooms where they had been playing computer games under cover of homework.

'Where's Dad?' demanded Matthew.

'Mum, you're crying!' exclaimed Jade as she ran to put her arms around Felicity.

'Dad's upset. We were all sad when Grandpa was so ill and died, and Dad's been studying for his exams, worrying about Aunty Paula and trying to look after Grandma. It just got too much for him. It's called depression and it can happen to anyone, but especially if they have had a lot of worry and stress. Don't worry, it'll all blow over,' she continued, with a brave but futile attempt at confidence.

'Hm, so what's Aunty Paula been up to now?' demanded Matthew. At twelve he had more than an inkling of the crazy adult world.

They never discussed Paula in front of the children, but she was a drug-addicted prostitute, fond of getting drunk and stealing cars which she usually crashed. Mitchell had driven his kids around the area where she lived, to show them where people ended up if they didn't work hard at school…

Damn, she shouldn't have mentioned Paula but it had just slipped out. 'Well, she's…she's…going to have a baby.'

Jade was delighted. 'Oh, Mum, fantastic. I'll have a baby cousin. Hope it's a girl!'

Matthew was stunned. A wise man of the world, he knew what prostitution was. 'Does she know who the father is?' he demanded. 'Slut!'

'Matthew! That's enough!' What do you say when kids come out with exactly what you are thinking?

'Well, she is,' he retorted.

Felicity let it go. After all, Matthew was hurting too.

'Look, kids, Dad will be back. He'll miss you two too much. He'll miss his home and his garden and my cooking…' Of course she didn't say how good their love life was, but held her children close and tried to believe what she was telling them.

But Mitchell didn't come back. He went to live at Paula's. He'd never been a control freak but his little sister could do to be straightened out. It's not easy to be into drugs, prostitution and car theft with a nearly-DI in the house. Mitchell's superiors understood the situation and let it be, as he could perhaps pick up valuable information from her. However, Paula threw him out after six weeks, claiming quite rightly that he was cramping her style, and even worse, as she was now obviously pregnant, the neighbours thought he was the father.

Now what? Lonely, depressed, missing his children and a warm body to snuggle up to in the night, should he go home? His mother was being cruel to be kind, she said. If she let him go to her, he'd never go home. Pride was his major stumbling-block, plus the feeling that he'd be putting his head back in the same noose. His work began to suffer. He failed his final exam, after earning distinctions all the way through. His weekly phone call home revealed that his children's school work and behaviour were deteriorating.

Mitchell went to work as usual, but had no heart in it. There'd been twenty millilitres of rain the previous night and it was still sluicing down. Eighty-knot winds bent huge gum trees frighteningly towards the road, with twigs blowing off and cartwheeling around the paddocks. He almost aquaplaned despite being pernickety about the condition of his tyres, despite his superbly honed driving skills.

Round the next bend he came upon his children, bedraggled and coatless, walking to school. What the hell…? He tooted and pulled aside to let them climb in, more excited about a ride in a police car, Dad's police car, than they were worried about the rain. He turned around to take them home and had just got up to speed when a ute came trundling round the corner on the wrong side of the road. Mitchell's reactions were quick but, distracted by children, rain, loss of sleep and worry, not as quick as usual. A head-on crash was inevitable. His airbags deployed, the children in the back were unhurt and Mitchell 'only' had shock, minor lacerations and bruises, but the couple in the ute were not so lucky. Mitchell radioed for police assistance and an ambulance before setting to work on their crumpled, trapped, barely-alive bodies. They reeked of alcohol - at eight-thirty in the morning? They were to say later how unlucky they were, unable to afford insurance or registration, simply out for a few drinks to drown their sorrows, weren't going to harm anyone, and they had to run into a police car. They were victims of the system for sure.

Mitchell struggled on. Oh hell, they were all so unhappy…and his Mum didn't need the extra serve of worry the accident brought. Maybe…

After three weeks of dossing down at a mate's place, Mitchell walked nervously up to his own front door and pressed the bell. He heard Jade's footsteps approaching as she called out, 'Who is it?'

'It's Dad, Jade.'

'Daddy!' she squealed. 'Mum, Matthew, come quick. Dad's here!'

The children ran to hug him. Best feeling he'd had in months.

Felicity brought up the rear with a wintry smile, and sent the children back inside. 'So you're back. I've just been explaining to the children about…Henry. I've…I've got a new man, Mitchell. It seemed obvious you meant it when you said you weren't coming back.'

'But…Flick…I…I'm so sorry. I want to try again. Can't we just…'

'Can't I just drop him and pretend things are just as they used to be, that this awful separation never happened, you mean? No way José. I've found a man who really loves me for what I am and I've never been happier. Sorry but what did you expect, that I'd mope and remain chaste for the rest of my life?

He stood there, shell-shocked, until brought out of his trance by another car parking in the driveway, his driveway, right behind his.

'This is Henry now,' Felicity said unnecessarily. 'I'd better introduce you.'

'Henry Pollard!'

'Mitchell Ross. My God, I should have guessed. I knew the name was familiar! Blackstone High, rugger team, Scouts… Whatever happened to you, you old bastard?'

'For God's sake, come inside. I don't want a scene on the doorstep. You're advertising the situation to the whole neighbourhood!' groaned Felicity as the children reappeared, Jade looking worried, Matthew smirking in anticipation of a showdown.

The two old mates started on the beer and began discussing Saturday's game. Felicity, redundant, went to bed in tears, Jade shadowing her. Matthew hung around, hoping to be party to Secret Men's Business, until his father told him to go look after Jade.

'You've only just come back and already you're bossing me around!' retorted the boy.

Mitchell let the insolence go because the kid was right, damn him. He fingered his service revolver, but whether to use it on himself, Pollard or the lot of them, he couldn't decide.

'Look, Buddy,' began Pollard, 'this has only been going on for about three weeks. If you really want them back, I can walk away and leave you to it. Option 2? I just left my wife, kids grown up, no baggage. You can have her if you want. 26 Boundary Road. Tell her I sent you.'

Mitchell's cold fury rose slowly in his gut like acid reflux. An old mate offering him his cast-off wife, willing to just waltz away from his dear Flick whom he'd professed to love, and give her back like a borrowed toy?

Jade came in, ran to her daddy and clung to his hand. Matthew stood in the doorway, wondering if this old mate of Dad's was going to hang around and keep trying to be his 'new dad'. Felicity, unable to settle, had returned to within earshot.

'You bastards, debating my future as if I were a pet dog or something. Get out, the pair of you. *Get out!*'

Henry waited, a bemused expression on his face. Mitchell felt dizzy, nauseous and helpless. He sat down. The children cried. Felicity put an arm around each of them and led them away.

'You heard what she said, Pollard,' Mitchell said quietly but with fists clenched. 'I don't want your rejects, and perhaps if you'll leave us alone I'll stand half a chance of getting my wife back.' He blinked away tears, thinking of his kids mostly.

Pollard left without a word, and Mitchell went to mend his fences.

Heart, Diamond, Club, Spade

Eric and Marni met at a Young Farmers' Club dance. They were both keen members, which worried Marni's parents, Edna and George, as they knew of a Young Farmer who had become pregnant to another member. All Young Farmers were bad news.

'You don't want to get too serious with that Eric,' Edna had said. 'You stick to your career. He's only a farm labourer and he'll land you with a houseful of kids he can't keep. Don't come home here pregnant.'

Marni and Eric carried on regardless, and a year later announced their engagement. George tutted, Edna nearly fainted, a not infrequent ploy of hers when things did not go her way.

'You're not,' she sobbed. 'He's a nice enough lad, but…'

'But nothing, Mum. He's a hard worker and intelligent, he loves farming and it's not his fault his dad's not a farmer. As well as being foreman at Grangers, he has his own pigs, poultry and store cattle at home, and he went to ag. college and got his diplomas. For goodness sake stop being such a snob and give him a chance!'

They married a year later. Things were not easy financially, and Marni planned to continue working until children arrived. She was not the sort of girl who needed her hair done professionally every week, or a new handbag every time she bought shoes. She happened to look terrific whether she was in bathers, ball gown or boiler suit.

Marni's colleagues at her laboratory were unfortunately tarred with the same brush as her mother. The men were up and coming industrial chemists or administrators, the women were technical assistants or office girls, but married suitably to young professional gentlemen. Marni and Eric did not fit. Snide remarks were made behind hands, lunch tables were always full or remaining seats reserved, invitations to company social functions not forthcoming. It was beside the point that Marni and Eric did not want to go anyway; what hurt was not being invited.

Marni escaped this situation when she became pregnant after six months. They were both overjoyed.

'We'll miss your salary, love, but we'll manage. We have a rent-free house, free firewood, eggs and vegetables off the property, and our own stock. And David's a good boss,' he said.

Eric had a heart of gold. Theirs was the perfect love nest.

Tragedy struck when Marni was six months gone – with twins. Eric was baling hay in the far paddock at Granger's when the machine unaccountably stopped. He was on cloud nine about the babies, not concentrating, took a risk and plunged his hand into the works, aiming to free whatever was jamming. He succeeded all too suddenly, and the machine refused to relinquish his arm, dragging him into itself.

Three hours later when Eric had not returned, David Granger went looking. He saw a bloodied bale from a distance and ran…to find Eric, dismembered and partially baled up with the hay.

Marni was numb. Her parents could not find the right words. Eric's parents, despite having lost their only son, and the Grangers carried her through the funeral, distraught, clutching her belly containing all she had left of Eric. She went into a deep depression, and spent her remaining three months in hospital.

The birth of her twins did little to comfort her, and postnatal depression added itself to her woes. The baby boy, Damien, being the image of his father, only served to set her off sobbing again.

The vicar visited her, and she was rude to him before he even opened his mouth.

She saw the dog collar approaching and shouted through tears, 'Don't you go giving me the God stuff. Where was He when my Eric had his accident?'

'Mrs Fergusson…' The vicar expressed his condolences, admired the babies and said he'd call again when she was feeling better.

'That's good, that means never,' she muttered to herself.

But two days later the young curate decided to have a go.

He got off on the right foot by calling her by her first name, and smiling. 'Hi, Marni. Do you feel like talking?'

'No. You couldn't possibly understand.'

'You'd be surprised. I know about your dreadful tragedy, and I do understand. I'd been married three years when my wife was killed in a car crash. Drunk driver. So senseless. It was a long time before I could forgive him. She was pregnant too, but fortunately at least our little boy Jason was home with me.'

That shocked Marni out of her tears for a while. She was silent before saying, 'Oh I'm so sorry. I know I'm lucky to have two wonderful healthy babies of Eric's.'

So began a friendship that was the start of her healing. Within a week she was out of hospital and visiting Eric's parents and her own with the babies, Damien and Meredith. The renaissance was under way.

Her mother fussed over Meredith, smothering her with granny love. Maybe, just maybe, this little girl would be the feminine daughter she'd always wanted. They'd go shopping together, and play dress-ups and dollies…

Curate James began visiting her at home, always in daylight and accompanied by Jason, who adored Damien and Merry. Soon it was Sunday picnics, sans dog collar, and other respectable family outings.

Jason was now five years old and very interested in this growing liaison. 'Daddy,' he asked one day in front of Marni, 'are you going to marry Mrs Fergusson?'

They both went puce.

James said, 'One day maybe, if she finds a new husband,' but he squeezed Marni's hand as he said it, and Jason knew he was trying to stifle a giggle.

'No, I mean you get married to her!' Oh, children are so direct; what to say now?

But when Jason was in bed, James rang Marni. 'Marni…what Jason said this afternoon…'

Her heart leapt. Was she ready for what she knew was coming next? This was a good man, a rare diamond, but… She liked him, for sure, but no one could ever replace Eric. Was it fair to re-marry? And her, marrying a man of the cloth? It was laughable.

'He's ready for a new mum, and I know I'm more than ready for a new wife!'

She parried. 'Oh. And have you someone in mind?'

'Oh, come on, Marni, you know I'm fond of you, just never had the chance to show it, you know what I mean, in my calling…'

'I'll…I'll have to think about it. Come round tomorrow afternoon if you can and we'll talk. But James…thank you. Thank you whichever way it goes.'

Her head spun. Eric had been gone barely a year and she would never stop grieving for him or reliving his terrible end. But James had helped her fight her depression, and did not ram religion down her throat. They'd had good times together. But did she love him? Could she love him? Tomboy, outdoorsy Marni, lover of farms and 'boys' jobs', how would she cope with being a polite and respectable vicar's wife? She shuddered at the thought of Mothers' Union meetings, church every Sunday, cake stalls, charity work… She was a believer, and would love helping with the Guides or Scouts, but…it was not the life for her. It wouldn't be fair to James either, in the end.

Marni went back to work when Meredith and Damien were two years old, not at her old stamping ground but as a chemist for a food testing laboratory, routine work, not too demanding, until the children were older. Each pair of grandparents had them one day a week, and for three days they went to childcare. David Granger had allowed her indefinite use of the cottage, but she'd had to sell the livestock, time constraints making it impossible to keep them.

Driving home from work one day, her car suddenly spluttered and stopped unaccountably. She had her head under the bonnet when the company secretary pulled up.

'Problems, Marni?' he asked unnecessarily. 'Let's have a look.'

Martin was a don't-get-your-hands-dirty man who knew less than Marni about the inner workings of the internal combustion engine, but it was nice of him to stop. It was dusk, she was alone, the traffic had thinned out to almost nothing, and she'd so far drawn a blank as to the problem. Soon Martin suggested pushing the car off the road, and said he'd take her home. It seemed polite to invite him in for a cup of tea, although she was sure he'd refuse, pleading the readiness of his evening meal.

After an hour, she tentatively suggested his wife might be worrying about him. Would he like to call home?

'Actually, Marni, my wife and I separated a month ago. I don't really have a home to go to. She took our little girl and…'

To Marni's embarrassment, he started to cry.

He stayed for dinner. He stayed the night. They got further in twelve hours than she and James had in twelve months. The relationship blossomed for weeks while they awaited Martin's divorce, but Marni couldn't bring herself to contemplate marriage; no one would ever match up to Eric.

When his decree was absolute, Martin popped the question one night after her children had gone to bed.

She was ready with her answer. 'Martin, you're a dear, you're so kind and….we have fun. The children like you but…it's unfair to marry you when Eric is still the only man I have ever truly loved. Can't we just keep going the way things are?'

Martin's reaction was a lightning bolt. He was not used to not getting his own way. People did not turn him down. Marni saw a side of him she'd never known. He swore, punched her, clubbed her head with his fist, accused her of leading him on for nothing, being a gold-digger, just looking for sex with no commitment…and left. Bruised and shocked, she let him go. She knew she'd had a lucky escape. She left her job. She'd had enough of men.

Time passed. Damien and Meredith started school. Marni, in between her scientific consultancy work with the Agricultural Board, now had to make time to be involved with school affairs. At a Parents and Friends meeting she volunteered to be on the committee to organise a fundraiser, bringing city folk up to enjoy a day on a farm.

One of the fathers, Stephen Spayde, was Eric's cousin, and he worked as a crop and fertiliser adviser for the Ag Board. They'd met casually at family gatherings since Eric's death, and she'd found him a kindly man, reliable, friendly and supportive. Stephen's wife had been unable to cope when their second child, Michael, was found to have severe autism, and she'd left the family.

Marni had felt oceans of guilt for keeping her distance, not helping Stephen or giving him any time, but she had no idea how to cope with Michael. Now they were thrown together by their involvement in Parents and Friends, he with Holly and she with Damien and Meredith, she'd have to front up. Michael by now was in a residential school most of the time but Stephen and Holly visited him every weekend. She began to go with them, to try to get to know and understand this little boy who was so disturbed, yet so brilliant in many ways.

Nothing was further from both their minds than a relationship. Marni blew her top when her mother kindly advised her not to get too involved with Stephen. 'You have enough on your plate with twins without that extra burden.' She was moody and preoccupied the next weekend as she, Stephen and Holly drove to visit Michael, leaving Merry and Damien with friends.

'Something's up, Marni,' said the ever-perceptive and caring Stephen, when Holly was playing on a swing. 'What is it?'

How could she tell him? 'Oh, just tired. It's seven years today since Eric died.'

'Yes, I know,' he replied, and took her in his arms.

As they hugged and cried, Holly jumped off the swing and came to join them. 'What's wrong, Marni?'

'I'm just a bit sad today, Holly. It's seven years since Meredith and Damien's daddy died, and I'm sad for Michael not being able to join in and enjoy what we all do. I'm OK, really, and thank you for asking.'

Holly had spent five of her ten years without a mother. Marni really did like Stephen. He was so like Eric: hardworking, honest and down to earth, kind. She could be a good mum to Holly as well as Damien and Merry. Together the five of them could forge a family which would include Michael whenever possible. A child with a disability needs a mum even more than most, she thought. But she wasn't about to propose!

Three months later Stephen relieved her of that responsibility. James had by now found himself a wonderful wife, and was thrilled to be asked to marry them.

Jason said, 'You see Dad, you did marry Mrs Fergusson.'

Fractured Fortunes

Jarrod Bailey slumped on the bench outside the principal's office, picking his pimples and twirling his lank, greasy hair. Sixteen, he ached to leave school, get a job, but how? TAFE was the gateway to that rarity, an apprenticeship. Maths was a breeze but literature was pointless for a motor mechanic.

His frustration boiled over that morning. He'd knocked over several desks and fled the room in tears. Mr Williams, the school counsellor, found Jarrod on the oval, sobbing, and talked him into going with him to the principal's office. She knew the circumstances of the hapless lad before her. Mr Williams assumed his fly-on-the-wall role.

'Had a bad morning, Jarrod?' Mrs Parker began.

Jarrod remained silent, his brain in a tumble-dryer, drying out with a jumble of anguished thoughts.

'Jarrod, I know about your situation. My job is to help you through this, give you some security at school, and help you avoid the pitfalls that are destroying your family. Now, tell me what happened.'

'It's all so bloody irrelevant. What's poetry got to do with fixing a car? What's the point of fiction? It's just made-up stuff!' he exploded. 'I just lost it.'

Ignoring the swear-word, she said quietly, 'OK, what are you planning for the rest of today?'

Silence. She waited.

'I guess I'll hang out at the plaza until Kylie leaves work.'

Mrs Parker considered. He'd be hungry and penniless, and would probably shoplift his lunch. 'Look, go to the canteen and get something to eat. I'll write you a note. Come back here and we'll work things out.'

Jarrod was pleased to comply with the first part, but didn't go back. He absconded to Robertson's garage and hung around the forecourt, all his bluster and most of his courage gone. A burly, blue-coverall-clad mechanic asked if he could help him.

'Yeah, I'm looking for a job. Is the boss in?' He'd get a job; they'd teach him anything he didn't already know about cars, bugger TAFE.

'In the office,' he said, indicating the direction with a barely-concealed smirk. They were used to teenage lads thinking they were God's gift to the industry.

The office door was open, revealing a harassed smoker, sitting among a pile of dirty coffee cups, cigarette ends and grease-stained papers, talking on his mobile. He looked up at Jarrod, then down again.

After an interminable two minutes, the phone clicked off and Max Jones looked up. 'Don't tell me, crashed motorbike, is it, son?'

'Er, no, actually, I… I want a job!' Jarrod blurted, sophistication evaporated.

'Oh really? I don't see any appointment. What sort of job?'

'Mechanic.'

'Oh, right. Then let's start with your particulars. Referees? Experience? Qualifications?'

Jarrod was silent, Jones not surprised. The school churned out one of these about every three months.

'Look, son, go back to school, then TAFE, have a wash and a haircut and come back when you're done. Off you go now, I'm busy.'

Jarrod stood his ground for ten seconds then, interpreting Jones's look, fled to the shopping centre. They'd go to Kylie's. Her parents wouldn't be back until eight or later.

Settled in his arms, she gently lectured him. 'Jarrod, I'm working to help out because Dad lost his job. I'm going back to school next year. You should too. You're such a reader, you have a terrific knowledge of biology, you could be anything you wanted.'

She was the only person to know about Jarrod's passion for living things. He did read avidly, not fiction or poetry, but not just petrol-head magazines either. He'd picked up a biology book in an op shop when he was seven, and digested the lot. He could have passed Year 12 biology when he was eleven, but couldn't imagine making it his career. He was equally knowledgeable about motors.

'Let me come with you to see Mrs Parker,' Kylie offered suddenly.

Jarrod slowly smiled, they did a high-five, then went to Kylie's room to seal the deal. Tomorrow was another day…

Kylie's parents returned at eight-thirty to find them eating pizza, drinking Coke and watching a movie, cigarettes and condom disposed of. They were used to Jarrod rocking up after school. Tonight he'd stay in their spare room, and Kylie would come to school tomorrow in her lunch break, to accompany him to see Mrs Parker.

*

'Jarrod?' Mrs Parker was surprised to see him with a girl in the uniform of the local supermarket.

'I – I've come to apologise for yesterday,' he stammered.

The principal's sixth sense told her there was more. 'Come on in.' She knew most of the story. She waited.

'Mrs Parker, I don't want to do English any more.'

He looked helplessly at Kylie, who rescued him with 'He's really good at biology and maths, Miss. He wants to be a motor mechanic or a biologist. Must he do English?'

'Everyone needs to be able to express themselves in their native language, Jarrod, even motor mechanics. You'd never manage tertiary studies otherwise. You'd be hurting *yourself*.'

Jarrod remembered his mum had helped his dad with business studies, because Dad hadn't finished school.

'You should pass Year 11 English. Then you could give it up, but you'll have to do a subject that requires reading and writing. Anyway, tell me about this biology. Do I gather you have hidden talents?'

*

Jarrod's father lay in his bunk in his cell, contemplating how he had ended up here.

He'd been operations manager in a company supplying spare parts to the motor industry, having 'worked his way up from the shop floor'. He'd struggled with business qualifications, to climb the ladder from leading hand towards the CEO position he coveted. He'd made it to operations manager when the infamous Global Economic Downturn of 2009 hit the factories. A proud man, when he lost his job he refused to apply to Centrelink, refused to let his wife work. Their mothers had never worked outside the home; Hilary was used to money and to the man of the house being the breadwinner. She resented not having her hair professionally done, and cancelling most of her social engagements. She continued spending, much of it secretly on alcohol. Whenever possible, she collected the mail and burned the bills without Magnus seeing them, but he was always around now when the postman came.

He ripped open an envelope, his face darkening as he read the contents. 'Hilary, what the bloody hell is this?'

They both knew perfectly well; the department-store logo was on the envelope.

'I just had to have a new outfit for your nephew's twenty-first, and we could afford it if you weren't so pig-headed!'

All Magnus could think of was the unpaid mortgage. She didn't yet know that the bank had foreclosed on them. He felled her with one swipe. Jarrod's little sister Jemima screamed and ran to her mother.

Jarrod didn't hesitate for a nanosecond, or he'd have gone to his mother's aid, phoned for help, comforted Jemima, anything but kick his father hard in the belly before running blindly outside.

There'd been a robbery in their street early that morning. A police car was cruising around, as if believing the thief would be waiting to be arrested. PC Coleman saw Jarrod running. Ah, there he is…but the distraught boy's body language told a different story. He drove him back home to find his parents embracing wordlessly, but this was the first of many such scenes.

Jemima started wetting the bed and stealing. Social workers came in. Hilary and Jemima were found a place in a women's shelter, Jarrod was sent to his grandparents. Magnus got six months for grievous bodily harm, and a restraining order was placed on him preventing access to his wife and children when he was released.

Hilary, faced with reality, discovered hidden strength. Under the alcoholic haze lived an intelligent and articulate woman whose first priority was her children's welfare. Her social worker found her a cheap flat, and placed her on an Alcoholics Anonymous course. She found part-time work where she could study and still look after Jemima. It would be a long, hard road, but determination to show Magnus drove her. Jemima would take a lot of mending; her life had been torn apart so suddenly. They both missed Jarrod, but with senior studies he couldn't become too involved in his mother's problems. He'd see them at weekends, somehow.

The shame of Magnus's incarceration was the death of his mother. Magnus was allowed out of prison under police escort to attend her funeral. Jarrod, Jemima and Hilary sat together, casting wistful glances Magnus's way as he stared at the opposite wall. Jarrod now bunked on the floor at Hilary's flat, and took two buses to school. Jemima cried for her daddy and Grandma.

*

Walter Shaw daydreamed from his office window, contemplating his career. Forty years in Bradman & Shaw Building Society had gained him early retirement with a solid pension, notwithstanding the global economic downturn that, together with global warming, was the reason for all bad things nowadays. Walter, happily married to Faye for forty years, a stalwart of B&S, a Rotarian, involved in many organisations in their little town, was healthy, wealthy and wise enough. His family were grown up, married, and had given him four beautiful grandchildren.

Not like the poor devil who'd just left his office. Formerly operations manager for Mason's Autoparts, Magnus Bailey lost his job due to the downturn, and consequently his home too. He'd been a member of B&S since he and Hilary had married, and had come to Walter hoping for a loan but, with no assets and a record, he had little chance of securing either that or a job. Walter feared Bailey would suicide if he didn't get help soon. Perhaps he'd ring Social Services with a general enquiry.

*

Hilary passed her business studies course with straight credits, and began applying for jobs in banking and accountancy. Jarrod passed Year 12 with perfect scores in biology and mathematics, scraping through in English communication, and was now at university studying environmental sciences. Jemima was scarred but adapting, as children do, and was excited at the prospect of high school next year. Magnus had a foreman's job with the council, thanks to Walter putting a word in to a Rotary mate.

*

Walter had retired and was enjoying being a grey nomad, until…

His mobile was on vibrate as he and Faye were on a bird-watching trip. He walked away from the group to answer.

'Dad? Dad, it's…Mark…he's…left me!' his daughter Deirdre stammered between sobs. 'Will…will you come? I'm…so sorry but…'

Walter signalled to Faye as Deirdre's voice gave way to uncontrolled sobbing.

'Darling, we'll leave in the morning. It'll take two days to drive home, but Mum can fly.' Faye's face was a picture as she tried to fathom what the call was about.

'Mark's left Deirdre. We'll have to go home. Seems he's been having an affair for months. Now Deirdre's found out, he's gone. If you want to fly, we'll get the ticket before we call back.'

Faye was almost as distraught as Deirdre. She'd never liked Mark, but he was a good father, and what about the children? What about the family reputation? Nothing like this had ever happened in the Shaw family…

Hilary welcomed her new client into her office. He had the opportunity to buy into a chain of women's clothing, shoes and bling outlets, a subject dear to Hilary's heart. They met frequently over the business deal, and began adding coffee or lunch to the proceedings. Inevitably they swapped stories. Mark was comfortably but boringly married. His wife was a poor-little-rich-girl, spoilt daughter of a retired bank manager, and Mark craved some excitement. Hilary had not entertained a man for over two years and this handsome, worldly-wise one could be fun. The business deal went ahead, giving Mark the opportunity to satisfy Hilary's need for feminine dress-ups – among other things. Deirdre found a package in Mark's car that was definitely not for her, a frilly negligee that with her upbringing she would have found too risqué to wear even for her husband. She said nothing, but then found a woman's brooch in the inside pocket of Mark's jacket. Mark, embarrassed and enraged, stormed out. Two days later she received his 'Dear Deirdre' letter.

Walter went round to Mark's office to confront him – and was introduced to Hilary.

'My accountant and financial adviser, Mrs Hilary Bailey.'

Walter felt sick, his mind reeling. 'Mrs…Magnus Bailey?' he enquired, already knowing, although he'd never seen the woman before.

'You know each other?' Mark squeaked.

'I know Mrs Bailey's husband,' replied Walter, tight-lipped.

'You know Magnus? He's not my husband any more,' the attractive woman said.

'So you think you can lure my son-in-law away from his wife and family?' retorted Walter, his voice rising, control ebbing. 'This must be your brooch!'

Hilary closed the shop door and faced the 'Closed' notice outwards.

Mark's Adam's apple began to wiggle, as it did whenever he was perturbed. 'Back off, Walter. You are always so bloody holier-than-thou,' he thundered. 'Does Faye know about your dress-up habits? Does she? Here, would you like something to try on?' he taunted. 'And do your Rotary buddies know about your visits to the gay bar? All purity and faithfulness in the sex department, eh?'

Walter turned greyer still, and slowly dragged himself out of the shop, a broken man. Years of upright living, community service and family-raising, destroyed in an instant by his despicable son-in-law. Would Mark tell Faye? Faye couldn't, wouldn't believe him – but she'd check. Searching Walter's wardrobe for the first time ever, she found the evidence.

*

Mark and Hilary escaped to the pub, where she had her first drink in years. They were beginning to relax, Hilary on her third martini, when three young men walked in. Hilary recognised one, kicked Mark under the table and turned her face away.

'What's up?'

'That's my son…the one with the goatee!'

The young men perched on bar stools, joking amongst themselves.

Jarrod turned round… '*Mum!*' he yelled when he found his voice. 'Mum, *put that drink down.* What the hell are you doing?' Oh no. His mother had conquered drink through sheer determination and AA. He'd learned about alcoholism through Alateen, and knew that his mum was now back on the slippery slope. He went to her table and addressed Mark. 'This is my mother and she's a reformed alcoholic. Was. Have you any idea what you've just done? And who the hell are you anyway?'

Hilary had not divulged her new romance to Jarrod. Mark heard loud warning bells and left his new relationship right there.

*

Jarrod had his mates drop him off at Kylie's house, where he poured out the story. 'Mum's having it off with this bloke called Mark Bignall,

67

who's left his wife and kids. I bumped into them in the Cross Keys. She and Dad are divorced. I know she has a right to find a new man but, Kylie, she was *drinking*. Bignall obviously didn't know about her problem. What can we do?'

'She'll have to go back to AA,' Kylie replied, trying to take it all in, 'but…we can't do much, except be there for Jemima.' Kylie was now a final-year trainee social worker, aiming to work with disturbed children.

They hugged, Jarrod's mind reeling. He'd been the recalcitrant teenager but was now a responsible student, thanks to Kylie and dear Mrs Parker. The adults in his life had all messed up big-time. Even his mum's new bloke's ex-wife's father, reliable, boring retired Building Society CEO, had unbelievable secrets. What was in store for him and Kylie?

*

Hilary sat in the Cross Keys, realising what she'd done. She called a taxi to take her home, forgetting about Jemima waiting at school, until a teacher phoned.

'Mrs Bailey, are you OK? Jemima's worried. What's happened?' The woman scarcely disguised her annoyance.

'Sshhure I'm fine, b-bring her home will you?'

Oh hell, surely she hasn't been on a bender, after all that effort. 'Mrs Bailey, can't you come for her? School has been finished for two hours and I need to leave.'

'Oh, bugger you, leave her then. I'll come.'

Of course the teacher couldn't do that, prevented by duty of care and her own ethics. Fuming, she waited. Hilary wobbled along erratically, but made it to school.

'Mrs Bailey, you can't drive your daughter home in that state. Put the car in the yard and let me take you both.'

Hilary, sobering slightly, realised she was back on the skids. Jemima was now thirteen, and went to Alateen that night. With Jarrod at uni, it would be up to her to bring Hilary back from the brink.

*

Mark needed a new accountant now. Deirdre still wanted him back, but her parents opposed it. She'd always obeyed them, but had no respect now for her father or his opinions. Mark had broken his children's hearts, and agreed to try to mend his marriage. Kylie had qualified as a social worker specialising in children's needs, and it came about that she worked with Mark and Deirdre's daughters. Hilary began the long, hard road back to sobriety, thanks to AA and strengthened by her love for Jemima.

Kylie and Jarrod married when he qualified. Jemima was a bridesmaid, Mrs Parker the guest of honour. Magnus and Hilary conducted themselves with icy politeness. What would become of this marriage? Had Kylie and Jarrod seen enough problems to help them cope with life's storms? They were idyllically happy now, like all newly-weds, but only time would tell…

No Accounting For Taste

The board met in the hospital conference room one miserable July day. The state of the accounts matched the weather. Corners had to be cut, if possible without compromising patient care, but things would have to be prioritised.

The buck stopped with Angela de Salis, the administrator. New to the hospital, brunette, one hundred and seventy-three centimetres (five feet nine inches to most of us), she had what they call an hourglass figure, only her hourglass was a little top-heavy, like an improper fraction. Her smart black work suit was always worn with a pretty, frilly, colourful blouse that was just a tad too low-cut, tantalisingly exposing her décolleté but only just. She always wore high heels that would send a shudder down a podiatrist's spine, and a tailored skirt just on knee length and not quite too tight. At work, her glossy black hair was always done up in a chignon. Her body language oozed 'Don't-touch-me-without-invitation', which was sent out to favoured ones with her hazel eyes, framed in black eyeshadow and mascara. Lest she scare off any potential suitor, a brain of great complexity and skill was kept under control, as was her temper, which she saved for unwanted ones. She was the epitome of professionalism except for the low-cut blouse, and all charm, sweetness and light on the surface.

The upshot of the meeting was that Angela was charged with reducing costs by ten per cent over two years as painlessly as possible, the sooner the better.

Charles Prescott, chief paediatrician, was at the meeting, having left his minions to deal with the morning's operating schedule. Tall and commanding, he cycled to work to keep fit and coached soccer once a week. A near-fatal cycling accident when he was fourteen years old had left him with a slight limp and ended his playing career, but at least he could still coach. The experience also left him with a burning zeal to help sick children. The reserved, cool, some would say stand-offish, Dr

Prescott allowed himself to scream and yell on the soccer field, even let the lads call him Charlie. He was brilliant and unflappable in theatre, delightful with children on ward rounds, but his curly auburn hair came with the temper traditionally associated with that colour. He brooked no nonsense from staff, parents or soccer players.

He came up behind Angela's chair and announced that he was not prepared to have his budget cut, she must make economies elsewhere. Not in my backyard!

You arrogant bastard, thought Angela, no wonder you're still single. If I can see wastefulness in your department, you'll deal with it and achieve savings like anyone else. 'Give me chance to do some reviews and feasibility studies, Dr Prescott,' she replied coolly. 'In six weeks I'll have reports from every department and do some inspecting myself, then I can start planning.'

'Wielding the axe, you mean!'

So the hackles rose, the cool, restrained arguments began.

Angela marched off to lunch, eyes blazing, cheeks hot, throat feeling constricted. She'd like to constrict *his* throat.

She met her new friend the speech therapist in the canteen and let go at her. 'Just who the heck does he think he is? Before the meeting's even over, he's getting his two bob's worth in first,' she fumed. 'I've a good mind to...'

'You're too new here,' replied Donna Trimboli. 'Leave it a bit, feel your way. Take it easy with him or he'll have it in for you.'

Angela scowled, and her quiche and salad gave her indigestion, not helped by three cups of strong tea. She'd given Donna her chips, to help her keep up the one hundred kilograms hanging off her six-foot frame. 'We'll see,' she said as they parted.

'Don't say I didn't warn you,' called Donna after her.

Angela went to her desk and put out a memo to all heads of department that she wanted them to scour their jurisdictions for ways to cut costs and report back in a month. This would allow for stragglers who thought a month meant six weeks.

Just as the tea lady brought her afternoon cuppa, her internal phone buzzed. Prescott.

'Miss de Salis, I got your memo. I'd like to see you before we both go home.'

'OK. Best you come to me. I'll be in here until five and you could be anywhere in the hospital.'

He bristled. He was used to others running around at his beck and call, but what the woman said made sense, damn her.

An hour later he was inspecting the inside of her domain, having checked on three post-op kids and blasted a new registrar in between. 'Now, about these cutbacks,' he began.

'You were at the meeting, you see what I'm expected to do. You won't lose services or facilities, doctor, but you will have to tighten up like everyone else.'

'Oh, and how will I do that?'

'Salaries are the main drain on any economy. Be ruthless. Have you any dead wood? Unnecessary office staff? Perhaps some domestic and maintenance staff could have hours cut. Do they keep their breaks to the official time allowed? How many toilet or unofficial smoking breaks do they have?' She wanted to add, 'Use your allegedly considerable brain, doctor,' but refrained.

He gaped. This was a woman, a new, intelligent woman, telling him what to do in his own department. His eyes strayed to the rim of the low-cut blouse. 'Yes, well, that's not up to me. I'm only here to do the best I can for the kids. My cuts are made with a scalpel!' He laughed weakly.

She did not. 'It boils down to voluntary restraint, or enforced economies from the top. A razor gang,' she added.

He changed tack unexpectedly. 'What are you doing about dinner tonight?'

She begged his pardon, although she had heard perfectly well.

'What's cooking?' he grinned. He was charming and sexy when he smiled, and she was thrown off-guard.

'I'm…going to a friend's,' she lied.

'As of ten seconds ago? Where does he live?'

'She. Why do you need to know? Are you going to check up on me?'

He put his hand gently on her cheek and ran it under her chin, lifting it so she had to look him in the eye. The approaching danger zone was avoided by a knock on Angela's office door.

She called, 'Come in' and an office minion proffered a bundle of files. Not everything could be emailed even these days.

'Oh. Sorry!' exclaimed Denise Marchant, a tubby student on work experience. 'Mrs Armitage sent these.'

Prescott glared at the hapless girl, who retreated swiftly. The awkward moment passed, but…Prescott had touched Angela and the touch had run right through her body.

'Was there anything else, Dr Prescott?' she asked, trying to regain her composure.

'Not for now, unless your friend cancels the dinner arrangement!'

She saw him out.

Left alone, Angela cursed herself for getting flustered, for enjoying the exchange, for lying about dinner, and for fancying him despite his high-handed arrogance.

She went home to her lonely flat, changed into purple slacks and a daggy grey T-shirt, stuck a frozen dinner in the microwave, put the TV on and sat watching it with glazed eyes, her mind back in her office. The microwave pinged and she went to rescue her roast pork and vegies, which she picked at listlessly. After Darren, she wanted no more of men for a while, if ever. He was an up-and-coming computer software engineer with prospects – and a wife and two children she'd found out about after nearly a year of his two-timing.

He'd left his mobile on the coffee table at her place one night while he went to the bathroom. It rang, and Angela had answered it to a child's voice saying, 'Daddy, Mum wants you to come home straight away, she's burned herself badly and can't use her hand. She needs to go to hospital!'

Mind reeling, Angela had said, 'This is a friend of Daddy's, dear, but I'll get him straight away. Tell Mummy to put her hand under cold water, and you stay on the line while I get Daddy for you.' The bastard! And what a time for his wife to find out about her!

She'd hammered on the bathroom door yelling, 'Your daughter's on the phone, your wife has had an accident! Come and talk to them!'

She heard the flush, and the sound of running water, before he burst through the door, grabbed the phone from her and ran off, leaving her to gaze at the empty bathroom before returning to the lounge room to be confronted by the half-drunk wine, their favourite CD still spinning in the player. She never heard from him again and she'd lost all her trust. Her self-esteem plunged to zero.

Back at the hospital next day, Prescott came to her office on the pretext of having a cost-saving idea. He asked her how the previous evening's dinner went.

'Oh…my friend had to work late…' she replied, with the assurance and conviction of a mouse.

'That's a shame,' he said with a barely-concealed smile. 'My turn tonight then?'

'Dr Prescott, I do not make social dates with colleagues, especially senior colleagues,' she heard herself saying.

'Charles,' he countered. 'Dr Prescott in here in front of others, but out of here I'm not a senior colleague. Now, will you come out with me tonight? Genghis Khan restaurant at eight? Or I can pick you up?' He took a step towards her to get a better glimpse of half-hidden assets.

She found herself remembering the last date with Darren, the lonely nights since, and acquiesced. 'OK, why not?' she answered him coolly, while churning away inside. 'Come and collect me.'

He went off on ward rounds, leaving her to try to concentrate on the accounts. The cardiac ward could account for every cent but was still way over budget. Her father had died of heart disease last year so she wasn't about to see them short. What about maternity? They couldn't kick new mothers out any earlier than they already did. She had a feeling that in the end it would boil down to being a scrooge with office supplies, sacking a few minions and cutting too many corners for safety. Charles would have to toe the same lines as everyone else no matter what.

Charles was operating in the afternoon, and one case took much longer than expected. Then a child came in with an emergency asthma attack and a hysterical mother. It was one of those days where delays accumulated until Charles was anxiously checking his watch in a way he rarely did. But then rarely did he take out such a prize catch for dinner.

It was already eight-fifteen when his Mercedes pulled up at the kerb by her block of flats. Mmm, nice area, he thought.

She saw him coming and came down the steps to meet him, on the pretext of saving time. She wasn't angry as she knew all about a surgeon's working life, but he wasn't about to see the inside of her domain just yet. She'd panicked a little, wondering what they'd talk about, but found him good company, humorous and easy-going, with a great variety of interesting conversation.

The Genghis Khan was one of those restaurants where you choose your meat, have it cooked quickly while you watch, or cook it yourself at your table, choosing your own sauces and accompaniments. Charles was a skilled cook and a connoisseur of the sauces, recommending they go back often for small amounts of different things. Piling the plate up meant losing track of what one was actually sampling. They worked their way through small portions of kangaroo, crocodile and emu with various sauces. Angela's napkin slid down off her knee and Charles dived beneath the table to rescue it, 'accidentally' brushing her leg on the way back up. Despite the electric shock this gave her, she kept her cool and ignored the incident.

During dessert Charles's pager beeped. He swallowed his mouthful of Black Forest cake, wiped his mouth and answered. 'Prescott. Look, I'm off duty. Can't Dr van Heusen handle it?'

The answer came down the line that Karl van Heusen was already attending to another emergency, and this child that Charles had seen earlier, operated on yesterday, was haemorrhaging. They were rushed off their feet and had no choice but to try Charles.

'OK, I'll be there in fifteen. Hang in there.'

'No need to apologise, Charles, I know it happens.' Chocolate gave her migraine and she'd settled for the cheese platter. 'Look, drop me home. I'll have my coffee there!'

'Thanks for your understanding. Come on, we'll have to hit the road.'

Home alone again, Angela cursed herself for agreeing to date a surgeon. Along with policemen and farmers, medicos were the world's most unreliable dates.

She told Donna all about it at lunch next day, but Donna was unsympathetic and changed the subject.

'How's your economy drive going?'

Angela groaned. 'Hell, Donna, we're supposed to be friends and not talk shop at lunch. I've barely started but Charles is digging his heels in.'

'Sorry. Are you going to the staff ball with him?'

'He hasn't mentioned it. Maybe he doesn't dance, I don't know. Who are you going with?'

'No one yet, but there's time. Speaking of which, it's time we went back to work.'

The afternoon dragged on for Angela bogged in paperwork, and raced by for Donna busy with children and their speech problems. She'd been working with a social worker, Doug Branton, in regard to one of the families, and he poked his head round the door just as she was leaving.

'Hi, Donna. I was wondering if you're fixed up with a partner for the staff ball,' he said breezily. He'd not long split with a long-term girlfriend and wasn't yet ready for a new relationship, but felt like a night out with no ties or expectations.

Donna was stunned. In her experience, not many men invited one-hundred-kilogram women to dance; she'd pretended not to care and carried on eating, a sort of social death-wish. Caught off guard, she spluttered that she'd be delighted to go with him.

'Right, great, that's all fixed then. Cuppla weeks Friday. I'll get back to you before then,' and with that he was off.

Meanwhile in Angela's office, Charles and Angela were having a difference of opinion about the old bogey, finance. They were interrupted by Charles's mobile.

'Yes?'

'Wesley, can you come over tonight, it's important. About eight?'

Angela overheard. The woman had definitely said 'Wesley' and Charles hadn't said it was a wrong number. She looked at him quizzically.

'My parents are staunch Methodists. They christened me Charles Wesley, and all the family call me Wesley,' he explained. 'That was my sister. She wouldn't say what she wanted but it stops us having a date.'

Angela fumed. She had indigestion again. This man who was such a pig at work wanted to see her socially…and she wanted him more than she cared to admit. She let the comment go and returned to her paperwork. 'Charles, your office is the most inefficient in the hospital. Many of the things you send snail mail could be emailed, ditto phone calls. Your phone bill is unbelievable, the laundry from your ward is excessive, so are your disposables, and there's a big bill for trivial things like wall hangings and toys and books. Get them given by the Friends of the Hospital! These are all areas where a little good housekeeping would save us a packet!'

Charles's turn to fume. 'Look, cleanliness is priority one if you don't want all sorts of bugs rampant. What do you want me to do? Use the same needles on lots of patients? And can't sick kids have something to occupy them, cheer them up? Don't tell me my job, Angela. I have enough on my plate dealing with their medical problems without having these hassles!'

She went home in tears. A full-scale quarrel and she'd only been out with him once. This business would drive a continuous wedge between them. Next day her resignation was in the hands of the board.

Charles got wind of it and came storming down to see her. 'What's all this?' he demanded. 'Why?'

'I can't work with you, Charles. Perhaps if we didn't work together… you know, I had a rule not to go out with colleagues!'

He closed her office door. 'Come here, woman!' he said, drawing her to him. 'Angela, please don't do this. I…need you here. We can work it out.'

Her jelly-legs went to water. He kissed her for the first time… passionately. They lingered a long time, she nearly crying.

Then, 'Charles, can't you see this is exactly why we can't work together. Please, I need to go.'

As it happened, she was head-hunted by Kingston General Hospital two miles away, and grabbed the position with alacrity. Now she'd see if Charles was for real or if she was just a convenience. She didn't hear from him for a month, and had actually been out with another man, Jeremy, a rather boring local photographer, in between. One day she opened her emails to find one from Charles.

'Sorry it's been so long. Remember that SOS from my sister? Had to go help with Mum. We had to find her a nursing home. Dad wasn't coping. How's the new job? We miss you here and the new administrator is not enjoying your job with regard to finance cuts. When can I see you? Theoretically I'm off duty all weekend. Cheers, Charles Wesley.'

She emailed back straight away. 'Friday night. Come to supper and rescue me from a boring new suitor. Angela.'

He was at her door at seven p.m. with flowers and a bottle of white wine, having remembered her allergy to chocolate and red wine just in time. She'd prepared a seafood salad, with crepes for dessert. She put the wine in the fridge and arranged the flowers in a tall cut-glass vase, a twenty-first birthday present from a long-gone boyfriend.

Andre Rieu serenaded them from a CD. They were becoming nicely lulled by good wine and food, and the perfume of the flowers mingling with Angela's Anais Anais.

Just as they were beginning to relax on the lounge, the phone rang, Angela's this time. Jeremy.

'Angela? Who's there with you? You're playing our CD!' he said indignantly.

'Jeremy, I have a friend here, an ex-colleague actually. I'm allowed to do that, you know! What can I do for you?'

'Do I hear man friend or lady friend?'

'Why do you need to know? You and I are not an item or anything!'

'Well, I thought we were, and that answers my question!'

'Jeremy, he and I, like you and I, are just friends! Can't you understand that?'

Silence. Jeremy hung up.

Twenty minutes later there was a knock on the door. Angela hastily re-buttoned her blouse, put on her shoes and straightened her hair before answering. She knew.

'Jeremy! Will you please leave us alone. You have no right barging in here like this! Call me tomorrow!'

Jeremy had his foot in the door. Angela called for Charles.

'Is there a problem, sir?'

'Too right, there is. What the hell are you doing here? She's my girl!'

'Get your foot out of the door and be off before I send for the police!' ordered Charles.

Police, my foot. They wouldn't bother with such a minor domestic, they'd just laugh. But there's obviously nothing doing here tonight. I may as well seek elsewhere, thought the boring Jeremy.

Cool, sophisticated Angela groaned. Two men brawling over her in her doorway! How many neighbouring flat-dwellers were watching, listening? How undignified!

Jeremy gone, Angela and Charles returned to the lounge, but the mood was broken. They finished their coffee in strained silence before Charles made his excuses. He thanked her and gave her a perfunctory kiss on his way out, promising to call her the following week.

For three days they both resisted contacting each other. Dammit, this was not working out; there was always something!

One evening Angela bumped into Doug Branton, the social worker from Charles' hospital, in Myer. Affable Doug greeted her with a hug and a warm smile. They went for coffee. Although Kingston was a town big enough to support two hospitals, it was small enough to guarantee being seen by someone you did not wish to encounter. Donna's sister, no less.

'Hi, Sarah!' Doug called out. 'Come and join us. What would you like?'

Sarah paled. 'Aren't you the guy that took Donna to the hospital ball?'

'Yes, that's right. Do you know Angela? She used to be our administrator but now she's at Kingston.'

'Oh. Hello, Angela.' She offered her hand but the look on her face told a different story. She didn't stay. Couldn't wait to tell Donna she'd seen her date out with another woman.

Doug rolled his eyes. 'What's biting her?'

'I don't know. She's probably another of those people who think if you have one date with someone, you're an item for ever. Just ignore it,' counselled Angela. She was in a raging torment inside, still trying to be cool with Charles.

'Yeah. So what about you and Charles?' Doug was so direct, so transparent and easy-going.

'Well, he's fun, but we're not getting very far. Something always happens on our dates!' she blurted in frustration, and told Doug the story.

He was a great listener. He was wearing half his friend hat, and half his counsellor hat. 'Maybe the four of us could have a day out together,' he suggested. 'Hey, tell you what, there's a mediaeval fair coming to Kingston in a couple of weeks, it looks really good fun. Do you think Charles would come? He must have one day off duty.'

They parted, and when Angela got back to her computer to email Charles, there was already a message from him. Her mouse-clicking finger trembled as she opened it.

'Hi, A. Just heard you had a coffee with Doug Branton.'

Angela's pulse shot up to a hundred, then she read on.

'Lovely bloke. Sarah couldn't wait to tell Donna, bitchy cow. Anyway, what about dinner at my place tomorrow? I owe you one. Love, unohoo.'

Angela only saw the penultimate word. Love. With trembling fingers she hit 'Reply to sender' and typed, 'Love to, Charles. What time? I'll bring the wine and my new CD. I bumped into Doug when I was shopping. We had a coffee and Sarah happened along but she wouldn't stay. Couldn't get back to Donna fast enough, by the looks of it. He asked if we'd like to join him and Donna and go to the mediaeval fair in Kingston the weekend after next. Can you get time off? We can talk about it tomorrow if you'd like to. See you tomorrow then. Love, A.'

There. She'd done it. She'd called him 'love'. And suggested another date. She knew she was feeling and acting like a schoolgirl.

They say tomorrow never comes, but it did and the date went smoothly, third time lucky, no door-knockers, no phone calls, but then they had cheated, turned off their mobiles and taken the landline off the hook. Angela stayed the night.

The mediaeval fair was, as expected, a lot of fun, and the four of them stayed out for dinner. Doug and Angela got along exceptionally well, and Charles found that Donna, the rotund speech therapist, was a highly intelligent, jolly, caring girl, not so feisty as Angela, maybe just what he needed as a foil to his highly strung temperament…ah well, we'll have to see what develops…

Out of the Frypan...

Martin came in from the farmyard one freezing cold morning. His three-year-old son Jake was making people shapes with the washing that was frozen to the line; both of them had red noses and could see their breath. Jake didn't notice the cold, but Martin was a sufferer of Reynaud's syndrome, which meant poor circulation and severe pain in cold weather.

That was just the start of Martin's woes. Raised on the farm, he'd known nothing else, and mostly loved it, but all those romantics and a goodly share of his friends thought it was all wine and roses, a perfect Shangri-La. On warm days when the crops were growing, the hens were laying, the little woolly lambs were gambolling in the fields and the machinery wasn't breaking down...yeah, right. Martin was depressed. He hurried in for hot coffee, a rest by the kitchen fire, and a chat with Pauline.

She was still battling with the ancient washing machine, and the kitchen was full of steam. With manure on his boots and his overalls reeking of it, he took her in his arms. She didn't object; her nostrils were full of it already, having been out earlier to feed the pigs.

'What would you think to us going out there next year?' he began.

'Well, it's all planned, isn't it, that as soon as your dad buys another farm near them, we'll move?'

'No, love. I mean Australia.'

She didn't answer, just hugged him as tears welled up. So he was serious. He'd talked of it often, this impossible dream. He was shackled to the farm where his dad would always be king. Dad the father, Dad the boss, Dad the not-so-magnanimous landlord, led to some tricky situations.

After a while, Pauline let go, saying, 'I have to get the nappies out.'

Their baby twins were asleep, but it was time someone checked on Jake. Martin slumped into his chair and sat gazing into the fire.

When Pauline came back in, carrying one frozen toddler, Martin was crying.

'Seriously, love, will you give it a go?'

Hell. She loved him to the stars and back, but what about her family? His family? Their friends? What would they do for a living 'out there'?

'Martin, this needs a lot of thinking through. We'd need a house, a job, a kindy for Jake…and we have no money.'

Independence was a big issue. They had a rent-free home, the use of a car, food and firewood off the farm…but a subsistence wage, nothing to call their own. They had little education, Martin's father having plonked him on a tractor at age seven and chained him to it the minute he could legally leave school. Pauline's father didn't believe in education for girls. 'What's the use of all that rubbish?' he'd said when she was struggling to learn her Latin verbs. 'You're only going to get married and have kids…'

'We can work, can't we? We can get to Australia for twenty quid, the kids go free.'

'Martin, we'd be running away, and before we do that we have to be sure what we are running into!'

They left it there for the time being. Pauline went to play with Jake before the twins woke up.

Somehow the jobs were done that day. Martin and Pauline were in bed soon after the children, the place where they talked best about big issues. They talked, they cried, they made love, then slept on their thoughts and feelings.

Early next morning, after a disturbed night, Pauline woke Martin. He really did need her to say yes. As well as huge problems, they could see freedom, independence, sunshine…and no more Reynaud's trouble.

'Darling…hey, wake up, I want to talk to you. Martin…let's do it! Let's give it a go!'

The next weeks were filled with form filling, interviews, medical checks, misgivings and doubts, interspersed with elation. Would they be accepted? No use upsetting family and friends until they were sure.

Eventually the letter came, confirming berths on a ship leaving Southampton on 21 July, their fifth wedding anniversary. Pauline and the children would share a cabin, Martin would bunk in with five other men. They'd be at sea for four weeks; ports of call would be Tenerife, Cape Town, Durban and Fremantle, and they'd settle in Adelaide. Martin let out a whoop and swung his crying wife around in a triumphant, joyful war dance. Jake thought his parents had lost their marbles. How would they prepare him for leaving the farm and his beloved grandparents, aunt, uncle, cousins?

Harder still was telling their parents. Their fathers were angry, their mothers wept, as did their friends. Good-hearted folk played devil's advocate and troubleshooter, but Martin and Pauline remained steadfast. Jake was getting excited; the twins would never remember their early months on the farm.

Goodbye day came. The truck bearing the exportable contents of their home had trundled out of the yard the previous day. Pauline's parents took them to the station.

Her mother pressed an envelope into her hand, to be opened on the train. It contained her gold watch, with a note, 'Take a little of me with you. Make us proud. Whatever we have is yours to share. Good luck. We love you.'

The journey to Southampton was almost without incident, except for the twin pusher objecting to being used as a wheelbarrow and collapsing on the London Underground, spilling its contents around the platform.

The adventure continued on board. As it was very foggy, the ship was partitioned into sections in case of a collision, and hundreds of bewildered, apprehensive migrants got lost on board, but from Day 2, the sun came out, people found their sea legs and their bearings, and began to enjoy themselves. After all, when would they ever again have a month's holiday paid for by the government? Martin and Pauline especially enjoyed mealtimes away from the children, who were thoroughly spoiled by the crew in a separate dining room. On-board activities kept them all entertained, and they could make friends with others bound for Adelaide, as well as making the most of shore excursions.

Their introduction to Australia happened in Perth. They walked in wonder through King's Park, heard a kookaburra, saw kangaroo paw and eucalypts, had their first battle with the currency, and tasted Aussie food – steaks, prawns, delicious salads that were more than a limp lettuce leaf and a tomato, and all so cheap! Australia was going to be marvellous. Sunshine and an avenue of Norfolk Island pines greeted their arrival in Adelaide, where they were processed through Customs and whisked off to the migrant hostel. That's where those who had moaned on the ship continued their litany. Martin and Pauline determined to take whatever was handed out, as it was a start, a roof over their heads until they found their own way.

Next morning at breakfast, a man with a notebook and millboard came in looking for workers. 'There's a job in a car factory out at Holdentown. Any takers?'

No one moved. Martin put his hand up.

Pauline pulled it down again, saying, 'Martin, repetitive indoor factory work would kill you. Please don't!' but the man had seen him.

'Yes, sir. Name?'

'I just want to know where Holdentown is, and how I'd get to work,' he replied.

'See me afterwards,' the man said.

The upshot was that Martin was to start a week later, giving them time to find their own home. August was still winter, but they found it hot walking the streets of Holdentown, with two babies and a bored toddler in tow, searching for a Housing Trust home. They found a small one within their means; not ideal but a start.

Martin started work, but on the second day the men called a strike, a completely alien concept to him. When the work's there, you do it, was his creed. This threw him out of work for weeks; receiving the dole was another alien concept.

Jake developed a bacterial infection which required four visits to the doctor, plus several courses of antibiotics. The money ran out. The twins were teething and developed nappy rash, exacerbated by the heat and unaccustomed water. On the farm they'd never had close neighbours, and did not adjust well to barking dogs, roaring motorbikes, vandalism and drunken fights in the street.

And Pauline had become pregnant again. At home (as they must stop calling the farm) this would have been fine, with space and security. Here it was definitely not fine. They needed to move to a bigger house, way beyond their means. How could Pauline work, with four children under four years old? Martin needed a job where he could work consistently. They ached for country surroundings. What could they do? Going 'home' was out of the question…to have everyone saying 'I told you so.'

Rescue came in a strange way. Martin's father died. His mother would pay for him to return for the funeral – when she'd work on him to come back. Martin thought it was a good job it wasn't Pauline's parent, as she was already very homesick and wouldn't have needed much encouragement to stay in England. Also, pregnant and with two babies too young to leave, she wouldn't have been able to fly. Martin left them reluctantly, leaving problems behind and knowing there'd be more problems ahead.

His brother met him at Heathrow, and during the drive up to Yorkshire he opened up. 'Mum's a wreck, Mart. Ever since you left she's been no good. Nerves, you know. I don't want to put the guilts on you. Dad's heart attack was caused by stressing about the farm, smoking and overweight, but his condition was exacerbated by your leaving. Too late for him now, but can't you come back, for Mum, for me, for all of us?'

'Don, I'd be going back to exactly what I chose to leave.'

'No, you wouldn't. Sure, the weather is the same, but can't you see, we're independent now. Don't get me wrong, I loved Dad, but we never had any say in things. You and I can work together to modernise the place. And I gather it's not been an easy ride in Australia.'

'Don, we're only just starting out, give us a chance! It took a lot of persuading to get Pauline to go and…'

'Exactly! She'd come back tomorrow if she could, wouldn't she? Especially now she's pregnant again. Boy, I bet that wasn't planned!'

Martin found his resolve slipping. Why would he fly in the face of what so was obviously right?

The funeral was terrible, ameliorated only by people's joy at seeing him again. He tried not to be emotionally swayed, but his mum was a big pull. When it was over, he and Don talked again.

'Look, Mart, I can tell you what's in the will. At this stage it's all left to Mum, but Dad said if you came back, you'd be an equal partner. If you stay over there, there's a pay-out for the years you worked on the farm, ten thousand quid. From what you've told me, I guess you could do with a bit now.'

Martin took a minute for this to register, then, 'Are you saying you could give me some money now, to get started in Australia?'

'I could manage about half of it, the rest when you've made up your mind.'

Martin called Pauline, but when she'd finished crying, comparing the weather and telling of Jake's antics and her pregnancy aches and pains, there was no time for Martin's dilemma. Phone calls were expensive then, mobiles not invented. It would have to keep until he returned.

Five thousand pounds! $10,000 in Aussie money. A bigger house, in the country, a better car. New clothes for Pauline, a tricycle for Jake, something for the babies…and warm weather!

Or…a partnership with Don, some say in running the farm, their friends and family close by, his mum, security for his growing family… but still awful weather!

It would be a long flight home.

Tally-ho Talisman

Major Arthur Crespin peered mournfully from the bay window of Oakden Manor. He would have been leading the Hunt, but was confined to barracks by a leg broken in a fall at the previous meet. He was dressed in plus-fours, leggings, tweed jacket and Sherlock Holmes hat, a pipe dangling below his handlebar moustache, the archetypical army has-been. His binoculars were in overdrive. Philip Reynolds was deputising for him, to the disgust of Miss Margaret Agnew. Couldn't have a woman leading the Hunt, preposterous idea. To make matters worse, his grandson was riding for the first time today. Miles Crespin thought he'd do much better without Grandad, who was such a perfectionist and treated him like a child, twelve years old though he was. As a lucky talisman, Grandad had lent him his riding crop.

Crespin saw the hounds charging across in front of the bluebell wood, yelping, sniffing, in for the kill. Somewhere out there was a terrified fox who would kill no chickens tonight.

Reynolds and Mrs Alice Watkins, a glamorous middle-aged widow, were the first riders. Miss Agnew was sulking somewhere near the back, Miles trying to stay out in front with the best of 'em but reluctant to use the whip. All seemed in order as they passed, and the Major repaired to his morning whisky while listening to a scratchy old vinyl record of Handel's *Messiah*. The church choir was performing excerpts for Christmas, and he was singing a solo, notwithstanding his cracked and wobbly baritone. Philip Reynolds was the organist and choirmaster and, jealously guarding his position as deputy leader of the Hunt, was easy to manipulate into whatever the Major wanted.

Mrs Molly Crespin returned from her shopping trip, and related the hot goss from the supermarket. They'd caught the fox, and Miles'd had his face smeared with the blood as was the custom, but that was the least of his worries. No, he hadn't taken a fall and broken his back but, worse, he'd lost Grandad's whip. He was back there now, minus horse, combing the course, in fear of his life if Grandad found out.

The Major, already fuming with frustration, erupted. Lost his whip? He'd give the lad whip if he came home without it.

'Be reasonable, Arthur. He didn't lose it on purpose, he was nervous on his first Hunt, he's only a boy, I expect it will turn up…' wheedled Molly.

'Carelessness. Damned kids, just plain bloody careless, don't value anything, just wait till he gets back here!!'

'If the whip was so precious, why did you lend it to him in the first place? After all, he does have his own!' retorted Molly.

Crespin kicked the cat and resorted to another whisky.

The hapless lad arrived, crestfallen, to confess. 'I'm so sorry, Grandad. It was an accident. I went back to look but…' He dissolved into tears.

Crespin clenched his fists by his sides and gruffly countered, 'I've had that whip since I was a boy. Present from my grandfather, family heirloom, yours when I die. Your useless father doesn't want it.'

Miles could take no more. Dreadful old man, talking about his own son like that! 'My dad's not useless,' he exploded. 'He's running the property and making his name as a writer. Just because he wouldn't join the army, you hate him! Well, I hate you and I wish I'd never seen your stupid whip!'

The old man exploded again, and chased Miles out of the house. Temporarily forgetting his leg, he collapsed in a crumpled heap and could only wave his crutches in fury. 'Get out and don't come back without my whip, you young scoundrel. How dare you speak to me like that, me, your grandfather, a Major and Master of the Hunt, how dare you!'

Miles returned next day to search again. About to give up and resign himself to the end of his rocky relationship with his grandfather, he heard a scuffling, panting noise behind a thicket. In a clearing, the strangest sight confronted him. Miss Agnew and Mr Reynolds, stark naked, Miss Agnew beating Mr Reynolds with Grandad's riding crop!

He stood open-mouthed, picturing them in church, Miss Agnew and himself in the choir, Mr Reynolds playing the organ. In the nanosecond Miles gave to contemplating how he could retrieve the whip without being discovered, Reynolds saw him and gave chase. The boy stood no chance. He was dragged by the collar back to the clearing. Margaret Agnew had disappeared. Like a dog chasing a car, Reynolds had no idea what to do with the boy now he'd caught him.

That short journey was Miles's last. Reynolds in his panic had inadvertently strangled him. He'd watched enough whodunits to know not to put the body in his car and drive it somewhere; he'd have to dispose of it right here. There was a pile of lime in the next field, awaiting being spread to neutralise the acid soil. If he buried it there, Miles's bones would be found soon… He'd have to be quick, and had no digging implement… He tossed Miles's body into the ditch and scooped lime over it with a plant pot from the car, intended as a thank-you gift for Margaret. That would suffice for now until he could think of an improvement. As an afterthought he pushed the whip into the lime too.

Margaret Agnew walked back to her cottage as though nothing had happened, but she wouldn't sing in *The Messiah* that Christmas. She would bring forward her planned overseas holiday, and never return. Oh, how she'd miss Philip! Mrs Reynolds thought it strange there were prickles on her husband's jumper and mud on his shoes when he'd only been to practise on his organ, but knew better than to question him. Philip was able to continue life as usual…at least for the time being.

Miles's parents knew nothing about the riding crop and, when he didn't return home, phoned the Major to enquire about Miles's whereabouts.

'If he was here, he'd have a sore backside. Brat lost my riding crop!' Crespin fumed.

'Dad, we haven't seen him all day!' retorted his anguished son.

The loss of Miles was the end of Molly's marriage to the Major. She could take no more of his arrogance and bullying of the whole family. Gleefully Crespin pursued his clandestine relationship with Alice…

Twelve months later, Mrs Alice Watkins, riding in the Hunt again, was thrown into a ditch. She fell onto a pile of bones, her horse bolting in pain and panic as wet lime splashed into its eyes. As she scrabbled to climb the bank, a sharp stick poked her in the belly. Fumbling to release it, she found herself holding the Major's riding crop…

Someone behind stopped to assist her, sending another rider to fetch the Major, who of course was out in front.

'Silly cow,' he fumed. 'Now the bloody fox will get away, what?'

'Sir, she's got a broken leg, cuts and bruises and lime burns. Oh, and she fell on your riding crop, the one you lost last year!' said the messenger.

'You mean the one my grandson lost last year… What, what was that you said?'

That was different. Crespin wheeled around and rode full tilt back to the spluttering Alice.

'Arthur, I think I've broken my leg, and look, I'm bleeding! Morning Glory has bolted and this white stuff is burning me. Arthur, do something!' she wailed.

'Darling, you found my whip… Oh darling how can I ever thank you!' he exclaimed. 'But where's Morning Glory?'

Panting, she told him he could start by getting an ambulance, washing off the lime, patching up her cuts and splinting her leg, and stuff the whip and the horse.

Bastard though he was, he admired a woman with spirit. He fancied he could hear wedding bells when she was mended.

Forensics tested Miles's bones and a verdict of misadventure was recorded. Poor lad must've been searching in the lime for the whip and fallen or something. There were of course no fingerprints. Philip just had to hope Margaret stayed missing.

The Manager

Gerald Morton leaned back in his office chair, eyes closed, hands clasped behind his head, contemplating his life. Not smug or self-satisfied, he gave grateful thanks for his luck. Thirty-five years in various branches of the same bank, twenty-five as manager at Springdale, saw him anticipating early retirement with lots of superannuation despite the Global Economic Downturn, which would once have been inelegantly called a slump. He was healthy, fitter than he looked at eighty-five kilograms, and married to a beautiful, articulate professional woman, Helen, who adored him. His children were doing well, and he tried to gloss over in his mind the fact that his son Peter was estranged from them. He was a respected stalwart of his church and his Lodge. Life was as perfect as any man could hope for, unlike for the poor bastard who had just left his office. Jack Mitchell was a hitherto successful and respected plumber, a tough, macho, rough-diamond Aussie reduced to tears by impossible financial circumstances.

'Morning, Jack. Good to see you again. How's business?' Gerald began, then wished he could swallow the last phrase, as Jack Mitchell's face told his story.

Jack was silent for a while, then, 'It's…well…I… Look, I know I'm one of thousands, but this bloody downturn has knocked me for six. Nobody's having work done, everyone's cutting back, creditors are screaming for money but my customers aren't paying up, I'm rapidly going bust! I never got around to making myself a limited company and I can't pay the mortgage. We'll lose the house before long. Janice… she's a dear but so extravagant and, between you and me, if I'm honest, a bit of an air head. She doesn't work and thinks I'm holding out on her when she wants more money. I just don't know what to do…' His voice trailed away as he averted his head to cover insistent tears.

Gerald steepled his fingers, looking down at his desk. 'Jack, the snag is, head office have put a moratorium on all further loans, exactly because of the downturn. I wish I could help, and I'll surely try if you can be more specific. Bring me your books this afternoon, will you, and detail exactly how much you need and for how long. I could put in a special hardship request and see how we go from there.'

Gerald came out of his reverie and started working on trying to help Jack.

Helen Morton arrived home that night in a state of high excitement.

'Oh, Gerald,' she exclaimed, 'remember that scholarship I applied for, for school counsellors to go to the States to share expertise with our counterparts there? Well, I've won a place! Oh, darling, I'm so thrilled!'

Helen didn't need to work, but she loved helping students with their problems, in addition to career guidance.

Gerald gave her a congratulatory hug, deeply sincere. 'That's wonderful, darling. When will you go? May, isn't it?'

'Yes, for five weeks. Oh, Gerald, I'll miss you so much but…I just have to go!'

'Of course you do. And six months after you return, when I retire and we're off on our cruise, we'll make up for lost time!'

Maybe, just maybe, Gerald thought, that would be the time to fulfil his great need. Their love life had always been good, provided he did not attempt to step beyond the bounds of conventional practices. They loved each other deeply, sincerely and exclusively, but Helen was restrained by her ideals, born of a prudish upbringing, with regard to acceptable activities. Who could imagine what might happen if they had a shipboard romance…with each other?

Jack Mitchell's wife was desperate. She'd not had her hair professionally done for a month, Jack had raised hell and cancelled her credit card when she'd bought a new outfit for her niece's wedding, the kids couldn't go on school camp and Jack had bought her nothing for her birthday. She had no qualifications for what she would consider a decent job, and was not prepared to do just any old menial work. Then an idea came to her, born of hopelessness and despair. She would approach an escort agency, not locally where she would be recognised, but in Brigham about twenty-five kilometres distant. All she had to offer were her looks, her body… Of course she wouldn't be a common prostitute, but a discreet professional woman catering to the needs of lonely professional men. And of course she'd change her name, purely for business purposes…

A fortnight into Helen's scholarship, Gerald had to attend a conference in the next town which involved dinner and staying overnight, partners invited, with activities provided for them during the conference sessions. Gerald loved showing Helen off at such events, and felt her absence keenly. He was intensely lonely and, on a spur-of-the-moment whim, dismissed his usual caution and contacted a high-class escort agency. Nothing sleazy, mind, not a common prostitute, just a professional companion for the event. Helen would never, must never, know.

Melissa, an attractive brunette, arrived in an exquisite silky forest-green evening dress, her hair in a chignon, false fingernails rosy pink, silver evening bag swinging from her shoulder, shoes to match. She had little conversation, but Gerald decided this was a good thing, as he did not want to get at all involved. This was a one-night stand, full stop.

After the dinner, he began to panic. What was he, respectable Gerald Morton, bank manager, Freemason and committed churchman, *doing*? But Gerald's fantasies were very strong and, after a few drinks and dances, proved stronger than he. Also, how could he escape? He knew Melissa would expect to go to bed with him, and he'd paid for the privilege. She was an elite companion, easing shy and partnerless professional gentlemen through their compulsory social engagements. Several of the attendees knew Helen from previous occasions, but it was a simple matter to explain proudly that she was overseas on a professional scholarship, and Melissa was his niece. Gerald was sure he'd be satisfied ever after, if he could, just this once, experience what he desired…although it flashed through his mind that perhaps during this encounter he'd learn how to persuade Helen, on their cruise, to sample these imagined delights.

The evening dragged on. The dinner was fine, but the wines were mediocre, the speeches were dry and littered with time-worn jokes, the dancing the desultory, obligatory kind. People began to drift off to bed before midnight, Gerald and Melissa included, pleading the hectic schedule of the following day.

In the foyer they bumped into one James Heggarty, one-time arch-rival who had made unfounded accusations about Gerald and some skulduggery, doing him down, climbing over him for a promotion. The unpleasant memory was revived in them both, but they made polite conversation accompanied by false smiles and too-hearty handshakes. As they parted, Heggarty's mobile phone camera clicked, capturing Gerald and Melissa's retreat as they turned to each other, sufficient to expose them.

Monday morning saw Gerald back in his office, regretting every second of the conference debacle. His panic and fear of repercussions had rendered him impotent, his dream of achieving his fantasies ruined. He could be blackmailed, his reputation shredded, his marriage destroyed. Dammit, he didn't deserve this, it was just…a whim, a brief aberration! If Helen found out, he'd try to convince her that nothing actually happened and beg her forgiveness. Maybe she was being unfaithful too? He felt such a rat, he almost hoped so.

All was quiet for a couple of weeks then, just before Helen's return from the States, the phone rang.

'Gerald, it's Jack Mitchell. It's…a bit awkward. In fact… Morton, you bastard, how could you? Well, you can stick your help, we don't need you, I trusted you… My Janice, I can't believe it…'

Hysterical sobs came down the line, and Gerald was not slow in putting two and two together. Janice. Melissa. He'd had no idea. But how on earth had Jack found out? Gerald had no inkling of Heggarty's photograph until he picked up the latest company newsletter, and there they were, he and Melissa slinking off to bed. Jack had found some work in Brigham, and had picked up the free local rag while he was there. The bankers' conference was a big event for the town, and there was a centre-page spread of photos of the delegates – including the self-same shot.

Another phone call next day sent Gerald close to suicide. His son Peter had been to see his bank manager, James Heggarty no less, at another branch of Gerald's bank. Both had rejoiced in the knowledge that they could destroy Gerald, that perfect, puritanical role model, that sadistic father who had thrashed Peter so brutally when he discovered contraceptives in his room. Gerald, philandering while his wife was away! Peter lost no time in gleefully calling Gerald to report on the photograph. What was it worth not to tell Mum?

Helen Morton returned from her scholarship somewhat subdued, longing for Gerald and wondering how he'd coped in her absence. They went through the motions of a grand homecoming, hugs and flowers at the airport, dinner out on the way home, an evening of her relating her adventures to Gerald…some of them, at least. Each felt the other should have been keener to have an early night; soon there was no delaying bedtime any further. They cuddled up, then let go and retreated…

Gerald tentatively began his confession. There was no other way. He'd prepared his speech carefully, but nevertheless knew it sounded stilted and insincere. 'Helen, my love… I've got…something to tell you, something that will hurt you very much and for which I shall always suffer anguish and regret. It's really bad, so bad I've even seen our priest… I ask you to believe it was an impulse born of loneliness, a sudden brief aberration, I was missing you so much, but in fact, although I don't expect you to believe me, nothing actually happened…'

Of course Helen could guess the rest and was barely listening now. Her deliverance, her release! When he had finished and started to sob, she hugged him close during a long silence, then, 'Gerald, Gerald, my love! Of course I'm shocked and sad, but…look, I understand how you felt, how it happened. You're human, darling. I can't be angry. We all have our weaknesses. We'll book that cruise in the morning! Meanwhile, aren't you going to make love to me?'

Gerald didn't want to see through what she was saying. Peter and Heggarty would keep, and tomorrow was a new day.

The Morning Walk

'Just going walkies, love. Wanna come?' I called out to my husband Mike as I donned my hiking boots.

We had exulted in the downpours of the last few days, after years of low reservoirs, parched land and terrible drought. We were enjoying the wettest July for eighteen years, but nevertheless were feeling like caged animals. At last the sun shone.

'No thanks, love. I'm going to get stuck into pruning the fruit trees,' he replied. 'Where're you going?'

'Just the usual, across Dave's paddock to the pipeline, up to the farm, back down Frosty's Road then home through the scrub. I'll have my mobile.'

'OK. See you whenever,' he said, pecking my cheek.

However, even before I reached Dave's paddock, there was an impassable water hazard. The gully had become a lake, so I had to re-route in the opposite direction…

Mike was a member of our local Country Fire Service, whose main task in winter was to deal with fallen trees and road crashes. He was pruning his third tree when his pager rang with the familiar call-out tone. A waterlogged gum tree had fallen across Frosty's Road. During the week it was difficult to raise a crew, as many of the men worked in the city. It took the few locals four hours to chainsaw the tree into manageable pieces and remove it.

When Mike returned, I was still out. He went to our workshop where I often fought with designer firewood on my lathe. I was not having a nap; I was not making literary litter in the office, I was not in the garden. Five hours she's been gone. Her morning walk usually takes a tad over an hour. Her car's still in the same spot.

He phoned such local friends as were not away escaping winter, and drew a blank. How could he have missed me? He'd been working on

Frosty's Road all morning! At four p.m. he called our local policeman. He didn't want to panic but night was approaching…

I wandered along to a cart track which cut through a paddock beyond the temporary lake, and realised I was close to a neighbour I'd not seen for months. I could use a coffee. In this part of the world you do not need an appointment.

I knocked on her open back door. 'Yoo-hoo, Pat… Anyone home?' I called into the empty kitchen.

No response. I ventured further then stopped abruptly, an involuntary shriek escaping me in shock. Pat was sitting at the table, slumped over. I went to touch her and the cold facts slammed into my consciousness. She'd been dead for at least several days; her slim body was suppurating and oozing the ghastly smell of death. My first instinct was to run, but then I figured any murderer would have been long gone. I tried to calm down, look for clues, assess the situation. Dummy, what's your mobile for? Ring 000. Oh hell, no mobile access down here. Calm down, Pat's beyond help, no need to panic, think… But what's that? Sounds like someone snoring!

I didn't investigate, but tiptoed to the door, nerves taut and on edge, prepared for flight…and slipped on some spilled dog food, crashing to the floor. I wasn't hurt beyond shock and bruises, but suddenly the snorer was standing over me.

'Let me help you up dear. There, are you OK? But what are you doing here?'

'I'm fine, but…I came to visit my neighbour and…' I dissolved into shaking sobs.

'Yes, it's a shame, isn't it? I dropped in to see if there was any diesel here. Did you see my four-wheel drive in the lane?'

It's a shame! A woman mysteriously dead when you happen to drop by, you do nothing but go to sleep in another room, and it's a shame? Foolishly, I told him I'd walked across the paddocks and hadn't seen his vehicle.

'I think I know you from somewhere,' he ventured. Feeblest pick-up line in or out of the book.

'I don't think so. I've lived here for thirty years and haven't seen you around.'

'Let's say I'm a traveller, but you went to Wattleton High.'

'No, no, I didn't,' I lied. 'I went to Springdale.'

'I never forget a face. You say you don't remember me, but there's nothing to stop us getting acquainted now,' he leered, taking a step towards me. 'Give me a kiss.'

I froze. What do they say? 'If rape is inevitable…' Utter revulsion filled my whole being. He could hurt me, even kill me if he wished. Had he killed Pat? How true was his tale of having arrived recently, looking for fuel? Maybe he'd squatted here for days. I'd fare very badly if I tried to fight.

'Look, my husband will come looking for me soon,' I demurred. 'Let's try to find some fuel and you can get away.'

He just scoffed. 'Come on, the bed's comfy.'

Seconds from horror, I steeled myself not to panic, try to relax and make the ordeal less physically painful. As he ripped down my jeans I realised I still had my boots on, and I wasn't about to cooperate unduly. Just as he was getting into his stride, an agonising spasm scissored through his back, rendering him immobile. My feet were anchored together by my jeans, but I raised them, kicking him hard in the groin, pushing him off the bed and rolling myself out the other side. Breathless from the encounter, I literally pulled myself together and tried to run, then realised I was going back exactly the way he would expect, along the cart track. If he staged a sudden recovery he would come charging after me, sick with wounded pride – and groin.

I took off across a paddock, scrambled over a fence that would normally have been beyond me, and sheltered in a small patch of scrub. Sitting on a sodden log to catch my breath, I suddenly heard a crack just above me. I instinctively jumped up but there was no time to move. The falling branch knocked me over and trapped my foot, but I was alive!

Hours dragged by, hours of lying motionless in a cold puddle with severe cramp, starving hungry and heading towards hypothermia. Eventually I slipped into unconsciousness, a welcome temporary oblivion.

When I came to I was amazed to find myself still alive, but for how much longer?

Mike had joined the search, combing the area where I'd said I'd be. It was a still, clear night illuminated by a full moon, which in our winters means freezing cold, but at least the search could go on after dark. Around two a.m. the sergeant in charge said they'd keep looking, and send for a team to drag the dam in the morning. Mike collapsed.

At ten a.m. next day, I saw a farmer out checking his stock in the next paddock. My totally drained, stiff and wet body suddenly became supercharged with adrenalin. I screamed with every gram of effort I could muster.

His dog came yelping over, danced around me, sniffing, then bolted to tell his master. I gabbled out my story to the farmer, who wrapped me in his Drizabone, gave me some water then ran to his ute for a chainsaw. Back in the vehicle, he had mobile reception, so dialled 000. The message reached the searchers just as they'd finished dragging the dam three kilometres away. The ambulance arrived to find the farmer sawing up the tree around me, and soon I was whisked away to hospital and safety. Mike was there waiting for me; we hugged and sobbed with relief.

Later in the day, as expected, I had a visit from the police.

'Madam, we went to the farm cottage where you say you found the body of the lady who was renting it. There was no body, no sign of the man you mentioned, no evidence of a four-wheel drive having been parked in the lane. I hope we won't have to charge you with wasting police time!' the sergeant growled.

I was stunned into silence.

Mike looked shattered, but squeezed my hand. 'You think she made it up?' he exploded, incredulous. 'There has to be something. Why would she? Why would she run across the paddocks when she could walk down a track? My wife makes up stories, yes, for fiction competitions, but in reality she's never told a lie in her life!' he protested. 'You get back there, fingerprint the house, find some DNA, look on the bed for hair, examine her clothes, examine *her*!' He'd watched enough whodunits to be familiar with basic procedures. 'And finding Pat's body would be a useful start!'

'Just describe the man again, would you, please, Mrs Parkes?'

I started to shake as I relived the scene. '..and he said he went to Wattleton High, claimed to remember me. I didn't see his vehicle because I came over the paddocks, and he just said it was a diesel four-wheel drive. There have to be tracks after all this rain!' I argued desperately.

'Excuse me, sergeant, a grader went through that lane this morning before you got there. It would have obliterated any tracks,' ventured a young detective constable.

The sergeant gave him a withering look but said, 'OK, we'll have a team check all surrounding fuel outlets, and another team at the farm. But before we do, are you sure you don't want to retract your story now?' he said, glaring at me.

'Absolutely not! And when can I go home?'

'You can go home, but be available,' he said frostily, and left.

Mike and I returned to the farm later with the investigating team. I showed them where Pat had been, where they might find her hair on the table or traces of body fluids. I showed them the dog food I'd slipped on. I showed them the bed, mud from my boots on the coverlet, probably a trace of DNA from both me and the man on the sheets. We went out to the yard, and found the diesel pump had been used within the last thirty-six hours, although the farm had been derelict for years, save for Pat's cottage. And there were Pajero tracks going right up to it. He must have taken a can-full, enough to drive back here to fill it up. We now needed to find Pat's body, something

I didn't relish. It had to be somewhere easy to get to and dump her, as the man would have been anxious to disappear. I didn't want to be there when they searched the well.

But she wasn't in the well. Under a tarpaulin there was a remnant pile of lime, brought in to spread on the paddocks to neutralise the somewhat acid soil, with a freshly used shovel leaning against it. Clever man! He'd dragged Pat there, buried her in lime hoping to decompose her body more quickly, but was not clever enough to cover his tracks. Footprints were round about; probably his boots were still covered in lime. At least they would now have to believe my story, but I didn't hold my breath for an apology.

A dark red Pajero was found a short distance away. It would not start. Its tank was filled with a slurry of diesel and water – water that had somehow gotten into the abandoned pump. A garage six kilometres away reported a man who had hitched a lift, seeking help with a broken-down Pajero, and buying food. He'd gone with the breakdown truck back to his vehicle. We were all waiting for him – me, Mike, the sergeant and the constable.

Triangle

Melanie Blackwell gazed unseeingly through the window, tears streaming. *Where* was her mother? She couldn't voluntarily have given her away…

Bella came into the room, all bustle and fuss. 'Get this room cleaned up at once! You are not leaving this house until you do, not if you stay in this mess forever.'

Bella and Don had adopted Mel as a baby, and Bella had never bonded with her. And when Bella and Don produced twin boys of their own, Thomas and Timothy, now aged ten, the world was watching to see if they treated them any differently.

'Mum, I…'

'Oh what are you howling about now, child?'

Melanie abandoned, again, any attempt to talk, and began sullenly making her bed. Fifteen now, she resented the 'child' reference. Bella left in a flurry of admonitions to chivvy the younger children onto the school bus.

Melanie frittered away the maths lesson, succeeding, despite her brains, in learning nothing. At recess she slouched across the yard to meet her friends behind the toilets. She accepted a cigarette from Jonno and sat on her schoolbag, puffing ineffectually.

'Wot's up, Mel? Old lady been giving you a hard time again?'

'Yeah, the usual. 'Get this mess cleaned up, whose is that ring you're wearing, if I catch you smoking again…" Melanie parodied.

'Oh c'mon, they're all the same, don't take any notice.'

'You don't have to live with the rotten bitch, Jonno…'

'No, I just have to live with my old man, who comes home roarin' stoned and starts smashin' up me gear.'

'Yeah, your old man's OK, Mel,' cut in Rick. Rick had given her a friendship ring. He didn't have a dad.

They bandied unfavourable comparisons about until the bell, agreed to meet in the shopping centre that night, and moved unhurriedly to class.

'What's up, gal?' asked Don that evening, as Mel played listlessly with her meal.

'You wouldn't understand, Dad.'

'Try me.' He smiled indulgently. He tried to compensate for Bella's coldness, and had tried to ensure that Melanie, his only daughter and beloved first child, was not pushed out by his equally beloved boys.

'Oh, it's nothing really.'

'That maths teacher been bugging you again?'

That would do fine for an excuse.

'I couldn't do my homework.' Then suddenly, 'Dad, can I leave school?'

'Leave school?'

Funny how he repeats things vacantly, when he's heard perfectly well the first time.

'Dad, I hate it. I'm no good at anything. None of those teachers understands what makes us kids tick. I'll get a job.'

Don leaned forward, drew a long breath on his cigarette and blew a smoke ring skyward. Aeons later, he passed the buck like he always did. 'We'll have to talk to your mother.'

'*She is not my mother!*'

Melanie slapped her hand to her mouth and fled to the shopping centre, where she collapsed in a heap on poor startled Rick, who let her sob it out.

A policeman approached them, wearing his wot's-all-this-'ere expression. Nobody spoke. Nobody moved. Jonno defiantly blew smoke in his face. Simon threw his Coke can towards the bin, and missed.

'Pick it up,' ordered the cop lamely, and moved on, at a loss for further reason to pick on them.

'Can't blame the fuzz for looking for trouble,' said Rick. 'There's been plenty of it around here lately. Let's go for a burn in the old bomb.' That was his mother's old Mazda.

Mel climbed into the passenger seat, the others piled in the back.

'Let's go to my place,' said Jonno. 'The aged parents are at the boozer, the place is all ours.'

They screeched away leaving tyre marks on the bitumen, scaring the daylights out of an elderly gentleman crossing the road, who responded to their V-sign with a shaking fist and an exclamation of 'Bloody P drivers!'

Several coffees later, on Jonno's lounge in Rick's arms, Mel felt warm and relaxed after the traumas of the day. Her plan to leave school sounded more attractive by the minute as she confided in her friends.

'Richardson's deli's looking for a girl,' Simon informed them.

'All I want is to earn some money fast,' declared Mel, 'to go look for my real mother.'

After an awkward silence, Casey ventured, 'Well, there are ways to earn money fast, Mel,' with a weak little laugh, attempting to break the tension.

In view of Mel's current vulnerable state, the others wished Casey hadn't said that.

There was a knock at the door.

'Hell! Who's that? Put out your fags and hide that grog!' panicked Jonno on his way to answer the second knock.

Before him stood Don, distraught after eight phone calls and three hours since last seeing Melanie. He looked past Jonno and there she was, sprawled out with Rick.

'Dad!'

'It's OK, love, you can come home now. We need to talk, you and I and…Bella.'

Hell, he daren't even say 'your mother'.

Melanie followed her father apprehensively into the study, where serious family discussions and reprimands always took place. Bella was waiting, reining in her emotions tightly to prevent herself yelling the usual 'And where the hell do you think you've been, young lady?'

'Mum…'

That's a start, thought Don. At least she called her 'Mum'.

'Mum, we were only talking, I had to talk to somebody.'

'You've never accepted me as mum, have you?'

Melanie was silent.

Bella played her advantage. 'What do you think would happen if you did meet…her?'

Don fidgeted, fiddled with his watch, poked the fire, cleared his throat. Sorting out trouble was never his scene.

'Mum, I don't want to hurt you and Dad, honest, but I know she would want me, she must have been in a terrible state to let me go. I just have to find her.'

'Supposing she's married with several kids and her husband doesn't know about you? What if you don't like each other? There are too many awful possibilities. It's in everyone's best interests that you let it be, but when you're eighteen, we can contact Jigsaw and help you find her if that's what you still want. We can't do anything until then, and then only if she has registered too.'

'Mum, I'm sorry, but I have to know. I'm leaving school, I'll get a job. I'll never ask you or Dad for anything. I have to know who I am!'

At this, Bella's ill-disguised ire exploded. '*You are Melanie Blackwell.* Can't you…' but Mel was already out of the room.

Next day she dressed in school uniform, but where her books should have been she packed her sandals, pantyhose, a purple sweater, and a flowing threadbare skirt which Bella hated. She was off to Richardson's deli. The job was already taken, but she couldn't go to school now. She'd have to forge a sick note. She disappeared into the city for what remained of the day, and was sipping a milkshake in a snack bar when she spotted Mrs Daley. There was nothing for it but to look nonchalant.

'Melanie! Good to see you. No school today?' Mrs Daley was lovely, much too nice to be Bella's friend.

'I…had a job interview.' That was not totally a lie.

'Oh. I didn't know you were leaving school. How did it go?'

'OK.' Then their eyes met. 'Mrs Daley… you won't tell…Mum?' Her haunted eyes searched Mrs Daley's face, trying to read her intentions.

'Melanie, we can't talk here. Come on, we'll go to my place and try to sort this out.'

At Mrs Daley's, Melanie spilled, shivering despite the warmth of her kitchen.

After a long pause, Mrs Daley asked if she'd spoken to the student counsellor at school.

'What could he do? Magic up my mother from somewhere?'

Mrs Daley let that go. 'Mel, what makes you think Bella doesn't love you?'

'It's just the way she's always picking on me, and fussing over the boys, and wanting to know where I am and what I'm doing and who I'm with every minute of my life, like I was a prisoner!' Mel blurted.

'Mel, don't you see, that's exactly because she does care!' The wise counsel continued, and eventually Mrs Daley said, 'Come on now, I'll prepare the ground if you like and ring Mum. Change back into your uniform. If you get your skates on you can still catch your normal bus.'

'No! No, Mrs Daley, please don't call Mum. I can handle it!'

Mrs Daley watched the troubled girl-woman trudge off down the driveway to meet the homeward-bound school bus. Teenagers need a trustworthy adult to confide in through their difficult times but… should she tell? Where was Melanie headed? She'd known her since the Blackwells adopted her all those years ago, watched her grow…

Bella was waiting, hackles rising, temper honed. No reining in of emotions now. 'No lies this time, young lady. Where the hell have you been all day? I know you haven't been to school. I found your books when I was cleaning your room, and rang the office.'

Like hell she was cleaning my room, fumed Melanie. More likely she was snooping for cigarettes, booze, dope, condoms or the pill, which she wouldn't find because there weren't any. Guilt, fear, anger and frustration erupted from her.

'Why can't you leave me alone, you rotten bitch? I hate you,' she screamed. 'I'm going to find my mother!'

Bella went white, and felled the shaking Melanie with one swipe. 'You go, you little slut. Go and see what happens to you, but don't come back here when you get into trouble, that's all.'

She left Melanie lying there and stormed off, shaking, knowing fear. What if some guy took advantage of her naivety, her vulnerability… what if history repeated itself? In despair she phoned Mrs Daley. When she came off the phone an hour later, Melanie was gone.

Melanie had run sobbing from the house, clutching her mobile and an overnight bag. She called Rick. 'Rick, it's me. Can you get your mum's car? It's urgent!'

'What's up, Mel?'

'I'll fill you in later. Oh Rick, can you come?'

'Easy. Mum got a lift to work. The old bus is ours, all evening!'

On the way to her best friend Cassie's, Melanie sobbed out her story. Rick lent her $50.

Cassie was horrified when she saw Mel's state. 'Mel! Come on in. Mum and Dad have gone to see Nanna.' She fixed Mel some supper, let her unwind, and open up when she'd finished crying. 'Look, you can stay the night, but when Mum and Dad get home they'll want to let your folks know you are here and OK,' she said.

'No!' shouted Melanie. 'Please don't tell them. I want to get right away, find my mother, start again!'

'So what then? Do I lie when they start checking out your friends? Mum and Dad won't. If you go now, where will you sleep tonight?'

'I've got $70, Rick gave me $50, I'll find somewhere. I'll call Kids' Helpline or something. They'll tell me what to do.'

'Mel, please stay here. Mum and Dad will call yours and tell them you're OK. Tomorrow, things will look better and you can sort yourself out. Please, Mel. Go and have a shower and think about it.'

Mel hugged Cassie and started to cry again, but she did go for a shower, then crawled exhausted into bed in the spare room.

Cassie's parents returned at eleven to find Cassie still up. They were upset, bringing the news that Nanna was very sick and probably wouldn't last the week. Cassie's uncle was staying with her overnight. That eclipsed all other news, and Cassie decided Mel's predicament would wait until morning. When quizzed about her late night, Cassie pleaded homework, which was partly true, her efforts interrupted by Mel's arrival.

Next morning she woke to find a note: 'Gone to hospital, Nan admitted 3 a.m. Love, Mum & Dad.' She roused Melanie, who still refused to call home.

'Mel, if you won't call them, I will, and I'll let the teachers know you won't be in today, but that's all. You can go from here, talk to a counsellor at Lifeline, CAFHS, Kids' Help Line, whatever, but you have to let people know you are safe.' At the moment, she thought.

She persuaded Mel to have breakfast and pack some lunch, sent her off to catch a bus to town, then worried about her own affairs. She phoned the hospital to enquire about Nan, then caught the school bus. She remembered Don and Bella, but left them to the school counsellor to deal with.

Mel sat quietly on the bus, her mind reeling, bewildered and anxious. She alighted in the city. What next? She went to a phone booth to consult a directory. Finding one not too badly damaged, she went to the 'Help' pages. Flipping through, a word jumped out at her: 'Jigsaw'. They were the people who brought together adoptees and their natural parents! She memorised the address and ran to their office.

'Yes, dear, how may we help?'

Breathlessly she gasped out her troubles: the wrangling with Bella, her intention to get a job and find her own mother, running away last night. The counsellor just listened, then reflected back the gist of her story. She'd heard it all before, another unresolved eternal triangle.

When Melanie concurred, she continued, 'So, what are you going to do today? Now? Tonight? How far have you thought this through, Melanie?'

Melanie faltered. That's why I'm here. You're supposed to help me. 'I...don't know.'

'How old are you, Melanie?'

Her hesitation betrayed the lie. 'Nearly eighteen.'

Hm, in about three years, thought the counsellor. 'Well, dear, we can't do anything until you are. Then we can check to see if your mother has registered with us. On your birthday, bring in your birth certificate, a photo and your adoption papers, and we'll see what we can do. Meanwhile, I do urge you to return home and make peace. It's a dangerous world out there.' She knew she was letting loose a disturbed child, a ticking time bomb, but Melanie had done no wrong and had a right to privacy and confidentiality.

Mel wandered into a shopping centre, a familiar refuge. Window shopping, she found several ads for temporary junior staff. She tried them all, but they were funny about her not phoning first for an appointment, and also why wasn't she at school? Drawing a blank, she went for a coffee. As she sat outside the café, a young man came to her table and struck up the most innocent conversation. Of course she knew about strange men, sex, drugs and all that, but this man was so obviously OK. He said he could get her a job if she liked, working in a snack bar from five p.m. until midnight. Lots of kids did it at weekends and after school, and she could start that day. Uniform provided, pay at the end of the week, a flat above the shop where she could stay until she found somewhere. She couldn't wait until five. She found the work easy, but was very glad to see midnight after her harrowing twenty-four hours. She crawled upstairs to bed…and found the man there, waiting for her, smiling.

'Hi, Melanie. How did it go? Get on all right with my other staff? Customers behave?'

'Er…yes, yes thanks, Marco, but… I'm really tired. I'd like to go to bed now, please.'

'Terrific, so would I! You can give me my reward for finding you a job!'

Her blood ran cold. All Bella's warnings surfaced in her mind, tales of raped teenagers, kidnappings, drug deaths… She tried to scream but no sound came out.

As he approached her she pleaded, 'No, please, I didn't expect… Marco, I'm a virgin, don't hurt me…' as his hand clamped across her mouth.

He dragged her to the bed and, when it was over, left her.

She sobbed herself to sleep, deciding she was now probably safer there than on the street. Next morning she showered, took breakfast and lunch from his supplies, and was gone before six o'clock. She encountered a tramp sleeping off the previous night's binge, another drunk rousing himself from a pool of vomit. Outside a massage parlour, a lady of the night loitered, presumably hoping for one last customer… or was she the start of the day shift? Didn't men make appointments these days, and the ladies wait inside?

The woman approached her. 'Want a job, luv? Three girls are sick, you've got a good body, the pay is good, what do you think?'

Melanie shrank back in horror.

The woman went on, 'I can get you hash, ice, crack, anything you want.'

Melanie fled. She'd have to find somewhere to stay before tonight. Frightened, she sat on the steps outside the CAFHS offices, waiting for opening time.

'I'm…looking for a foster home,' she told the receptionist lamely.

She was told to wait for a counsellor. Same rigmarole as at Jigsaw. Don't these people understand?

'Melanie, foster homes are for youngsters who come from dangerous homes with drunken fathers who abuse them, kids who've been in trouble with the law, or have no home at all, and we are so short of foster-parents for those cases. I'm sorry, but you've no chance of getting one even if you make yourself a ward of the state, which you can at fifteen. Then you have to live where we say, you can't go home if you change your mind.' She didn't add that foster homes have rules too.

'But I can't go home!' wailed Mel. 'They wouldn't want me back anyway.'

In despair, she ran out of the office, to wander the streets all day.

When the shopping and work crowds had gone and evening theatregoers were arriving, she went into a park. A park bench was preferable to a shop doorway, stairwell or under a bridge for the night. She daren't spend her money; one night's accommodation would take the lot. She met a young couple, must have been all of sixteen, and accepted a cigarette from them, her first for forty-eight hours.

They laughed as they talked. 'Hey look, we're street kids. Gets a bit cold at night but we've found somewhere. Lots of us use an empty warehouse. We get the dole, it buys our tucker and fags, and there's plenty of department stores who are very careless with their displays… Wanna come?' They offered her a joint which she felt obliged to take, wondering fleetingly where her life was going.

The warehouse was marginally less cold than the park. A rosy marijuana-induced haze overtook her and she didn't care about anything.

This came to an abrupt end at about two a.m. A fire had broken out in the warehouse. Melanie awoke to the sound of crackling flames and wracking coughs due to smoke inhalation. She got up and ran, giving her new companions a shove as she climbed over others, screaming at them to get going. She tripped at the entrance, collapsing unconscious as she banged her head on a concrete pillar. A fireman dragged her out to a waiting ambulance. At the hospital, police were waiting to interview all warehouse-dwellers who were still alive but had failed to evade them, Melanie Blackwell included…

'Whatever possessed you, love?' asked Don gently, sitting by her bed, holding her hand.

'Dad, Bella doesn't love me, never has. I have to know who I am, have to meet…her, you know…'

'That's not true, Mel. Bella loves you all to high heaven, and she doesn't deserve this. When you're eighteen we'll help you, but you'll just have to live with the not-knowing until then, I'm afraid. Promise me you'll come home and live with us at least until you're eighteen. Please, love. You've found out the hard way what a tough world it is out there.'

She squeezed his hand. 'Just leave it for now, Dad. I'm tired, so tired. I can't talk any more.'

A nurse came to ask Don to leave.

Bella was at home with Tom and Tim, wondering how it would be if and when Melanie came home. Could they make it work? She was willing, but Mel would have to toe a few lines. It would be easy to let her get away with things as a sort of bribe to get her to stay, but that wouldn't do. They'd need a big family conference, preferably with a disinterested party present. She called Mrs Daley.

When Don brought Mel home a week later, Mrs Daley and Bella were waiting, with two nosey little boys hanging around in the doorway.

'Is our Mel in trouble, Dad?' asked Tim.

'She's had a tough time Tim, and we need to talk about it. You two buzz off and do your homework or something, just give us an hour, OK?'

Tim and Tom gave each other meaningful looks but drifted off, wondering if they'd be able to hear the conversation from a safe distance.

Mel blanched when she saw Mrs Daley. 'You said you wouldn't tell, I trusted you!' she exploded.

'Mel, I didn't tell, but if I had, I might have saved you all this trouble,' she replied gently. 'I want to help you and your family sort this out if I can.'

'OK, Mel, from the beginning, tell us what happened.' For once Don was picking up his fatherly role.

Mel started to cry as she related events. There was a long silence when she'd finished.

'What do *you* want to happen now, Mel?' asked Mrs Daley.

This startled Mel, who did not think she'd have any say, as usual. After a while she ventured, 'I'd just like…Mum and me…to be sort of adult friends. Truly I don't want to hurt her, I want her to love me… but not like she loves Tim and Tom. They're just kids and I'm nearly grown up. I can drive in three months' time and…' she stopped short of saying she'd be legally old enough for sex too '…and…Mum…I shouldn't have called you a bitch. I know I've been a bit of a bitch myself but only because…' she drifted off.

Bella's turn. 'And I'm sorry I hit you, but I was at my wits' end, I just didn't know what to do to make you see sense! There'll have to be some changes, Melanie. You'll have to act like an adult if that's what you want. You can't be a child when it suits you, and at the same time have the privileges of being an adult. While you live with us you'll have to help with chores and things, and go to school and do your best and obey the rules. Dad and I work hard to give you three a good home and a good education and you must start to see school as your work, your preparation for your future. In the end you are the one who will benefit, not us.'

The four of them discussed a plan that they all thought would work; rules, privileges, freedoms, expectations… Mrs Daley went home. Don went off to see what the boys were up to, leaving Bella and Mel to talk.

The cold, immutable Bella hugged Mel and they both cried. Catharsis! This should have happened years ago…but Mel wasn't a disturbed teenager years ago. What a pity she had to go through forty-eight hours of hell and a week in hospital to come to the realisation she was loved. What a pity Bella did not then understand the uneven development of the teenage brain, and the torment that this, and hormones, bring to the adolescent. Triangle resolved.

Up In Smoke

Brad Baxter and Scott Markham, now captains of their respective Country Fire Service brigades, were reminiscing over a beer in the Wattleton Arms. Grown men now with teenage lads of their own, they well remembered their exploits back in 1980.

'D'you remember when they used to cane us for smoking!' laughed Brad. 'Imagine that now!'

'Yeah, we thought it was a huge joke, especially when it was someone else! Then they had the bright idea of a smoking room – we called it the Smokehouse – where you could have a fag during breaks if you brought a note! Those who couldn't forge a parent's signature soon learned,' grinned Scott.

Then their faces darkened, their voices trailing away as they remembered the rest.

Scott and Brad had been top dogs in the Smokehouse until it got too public for their main agenda.

'Brad, c'mon, we've got stuff to discuss,' began Scott one day on their way to the Smokehouse. 'Can't talk in there. Let's have a walk around the oval.'

At the end of the oval was a patch of hilly scrub.

When the bell rang, Scott grabbed Brad's arm as he turned to go. 'C'mon, got stuff to show you.'

They disappeared into the scrub, where Scott had been on a CFS exercise the previous evening. The boys were proud of their new status as qualified firemen, Scott at Wattleton and Brad under his dad's tutelage at Springdale.

'Look!' Brad bent down and saw the disturbed earth, as though a dog had been burying a bone. His fingers found a small wooden slab serving as a door. 'What is it?' he said, heart thumping. 'Can we go in and have a look?'

'Nothing stopping us,' grinned Scott, and led the way into a concrete-lined bunker about four metres square. 'Found it last night! Dunno who knows about it, if anybody! We could bring the dope here. Only our clients would know. We'll only come out of school hours, in the dark. C'mon, we'd better get back.'

They had different classes, so a conspiracy would go unnoticed. 'Sorry, sir, couldn't find my books.' Probing by Sir would only disrupt the class further.

At lunchtime they buttonholed their marijuana clients individually.

'Meet us on the oval at seven p.m. tomorrow. Come alone, tell no one' was the cryptic message, perfectly understood.

At the appointed time, Brad and Scott led the little procession down into the bunker.

Conjecture flared – was it a wartime relic, a cellar, a disused drug lab? Karen was scared, claiming that obviously someone knew it was there. Queenie shivered.

'It's not been used for years,' said Scott. 'The perfect place, but don't come here in school time, only with us after dark. If anybody's kid brother finds out, we're history!'

Scott saw his Uncle Max that night. 'Max, I found the perfect den when I was out with CFS. You get me the stuff, we'll do a roaring trade at school.'

Max Markham was under pressure from his supplier and employer, one Dan Butcher, leader of the infamous Butcherbirds bikie gang, to sell more drugs. He didn't want to start the kids on anything stronger than marijuana, but his hand was being forced. Max had done time for embezzling funds at the local supermarket where he used to be manager. He'd lost his family over that, and more jail time would see him permanently unemployed.

'Why do they call him Butcherbird?' queried Brad.

'Well, his name's Butcher, he's an ex-jailbird like Max, but also he swoops into a swarm of people, picks his victim and nails him, just like a butcherbird!' laughed Scott.

The enterprise gained momentum slowly over the ensuing weeks –
until the day the boys sold a joint to Queenie. She was the archetypical
Angry Young Woman – angry with her parents for her name – dammit,
didn't they know what a queen was? She was angry with her absent father
for being a cop and for leaving the family, angry because she was fat,
angry because she had few friends and, like most angry people, angry
with herself. She knew that being fat was both the cause and the result
of much of her unhappiness, the constant eating she seemed unable
to stop despite the teasing she endured. She kept quiet about Daddy
being an undercover cop, one with a twitchy nose that could smell dope
from infinity. He came home unexpectedly that night and beat out of
her what was going on, including the details of the next rendezvous.
When he arrived in uniform ten minutes into the meeting, Uncle Max's
trade route hit the wall.

Queenie was grounded by her father, and she, Scott, Brad and
others were suspended from school. Karen had been absent that day,
so escaped.

'But Dad…' Queenie pleaded.

Her friends were blaming her, of course.

'But Dad nothing, you stupid little cow. How do you think I look,
a drug cop's daughter involved in the stuff? You're grounded until the
whole damn thing goes to court!'

But then Dad was off again, and Queenie always got her own way
with Mum, who tried to make up for the separation and buy her off
from her father.

'Mum, there's a sleep-over at Karen's tonight. Can I go, just this
once, pleeease? I'll come home first thing in the morning, promise!'

Karen was a good girl, no trouble, a good influence on Queenie.
Mum acquiesced.

John Baxter, captain of Springdale CFS, rolled over in bed, checked
that his pager was on and kissed Margaret goodnight. At twelve twenty-
seven a.m. the pager shrilled. Margaret swore silently and sleepily. Now
what? More trivial information that bloody Joe Bloggs had gone fishing

or something? But John read the message. 'Fire at service station, Wattleton.' He was out of bed and into his clothes in seconds with a 'Gottago, luv', hammering on Brad's door as he passed. Man and boy were into the car and off to their station in no time. Seven hours later they were still not home.

John had a funny feeling about tonight. There had been a series of fires at a rented house belonging to Butcherbird some weeks earlier. Was there a connection? Plenty of people had it in for Butcherbird and Max Markham, who managed the service station for him. Anyone would be better off with the insurance money than a decrepit outfit in danger of closing down because it couldn't pay the oil company's upfront demands for fuel. The town collectively deduced the fire was arson.

John arrived at the fire station to find a full crew ready to go, and they were at the scene in eight minutes. Wattleton brigade were already there, other local brigades on their way, and soon over eighty local men and women were playing their part, having been roused from slumber.

John's attention was suddenly caught by Scott spraying water through a broken window, into the building. Everyone else with a fire hose was concentrating on the outside walls to prevent further spread to surrounding properties. The station was at a road junction and surrounded by houses, the school not far away.

John hastily grabbed Scott's hose. 'Scott…what the hell are you doing? Don't you remember from your training not to hose the source of the fire?'

Scott looked abashed. 'S-sorry John, but…why not?' he stammered.

'You can destroy evidence! I know the bloody thing's burning down, but a fire can leave its own evidence of what started it, unless some idiot washes it away!'

Sulkily, Scott mumbled something about only being a volunteer, he didn't have to be there, might as well have stayed in bed if that's what thanks he got.

Wattleton's captain came over to speak to John. 'That lad needs watching, John, I'm afraid, and I was round the back with the Hazmat team. I'll sort him out at training, but right now we've gotta get on top of this lot.'

The firefighters' terror was that the fire could get to the underground tanks. In theory they knew it couldn't, yet still they feared they were working on top of an unexploded bomb. Detectives were examining the extinguished sections. Scott was sent to man a road block, minus fire hose.

Later that day, he had a visit from Butcherbird.

'How d'you go this morning, boyo?'

'Look, I never set that fire and I've no idea who did, but I bet you do. Me and Brad were doing our duty, putting the bloody thing out! I gave it plenty inside before Brad's dad stopped me. I wanted to wash away the evidence to keep Max out of trouble because I know you keep the goods there.'

'Problem is, kid, I don't know who set the fire. It often crossed my mind, but I'd be Suspect Number 1. People do it all the time for the insurance money and I'm not that stupid. I'm not sorry, but I've got to get myself out of the frame. Trying to destroy evidence puts you firmly *in* the frame! Someone reported hearing a car leaving the scene but they didn't see anything.'

Scott couldn't wait to consult with Brad.

Queenie and Karen borrowed Karen's parents' car to go for an innocent little drive.

'Don't wait up,' she told them, 'We'll be back by midnight!'

Karen's parents trusted her. She was not one of the villains suspended for drugs.

Queenie confided in her. '…and they all hate me because my dad found out and if I can help them get off…'

'What are you going to do, then?' asked Karen, puzzled and not a little curious.

'Look, Max Markham is scum. He keeps the drugs in the service station where he works. If it got burned down, the evidence would be gone, so would his job, and his employer would get done for insurance fraud! I heard Dad saying the place was on its knees anyway!'

'So… Queenie, you wouldn't! Don't be crazy! I'm having nothing to do with it.'

'You don't have to. Just drop me off and I'll walk home to your place.'

'I can't leave you in the middle of the night…you might go up with it, or anything. Have you lost your mind?'

'Then just drop me out. I need to use their loo. They leave it open. Wait for me. We'll be back home by midnight like you said!'

Uneasily, Karen acquiesced.

Queenie had been following the modus operandi of a local arsonist. The newspaper had seen fit to describe in detail how he'd done it. It took her three minutes to set the device, and she was back in the car by eleven-thirty, lots of time to get home to Karen's before the curfew. It would take a while for the fire to take hold, by which time they'd be slumbering.

Next morning, Karen's mum phoned Queenie's mum. 'Jane, are the girls at your place?'

'Oh no, don't tell me! I let Queenie go to your place last night! Her dad grounded her but…sometimes he's a bit harsh and…oh Sharon, don't tell me they're not with you!'

A motorist going to work found the car in a ditch. Queenie was dead. Karen came to in hospital, battered and broken, but her head injuries were only minor. She was interviewed on the second day.

Scott and Brad plonked their beer glasses on the bar, wiped a hand across their mouths and sauntered out to the veranda, where they paused for a last cigarette.

'Yeah, it was a tragic night. Can't believe we were mixed up in it. Queenie was a strange girl but we were all responsible. We gave her such a hard time.'

'It was a helluva lesson. Ah well, I wonder what we'll learn about Jake and Cody at parent interviews tomorrow?'

Both rolled their eyes skyward.

'At least I don't think they smoke,' said Brad, 'neither nicotine nor dope!' They hopped into their utes and trundled off home.

Refugee

I'm South Australia's 2025 Rhodes Scholar. I was sitting in a lecture hall here at Queen's College, Oxford, as debate was raging about illegal immigrants to the UK. My mind began to wander soon after the start.

The year was 2010. I was ten years old, newly arrived on a leaky boat with my family – or those who were left of it. My father had been killed in Afghanistan. My baby sister had died during our perilous journey to escape torture and death. My mother and older sister were among hundreds of women routinely gang raped by the Taliban. I do not know what happened to my sister. Mother escaped with me and my two younger brothers.

We were held in an offshore detention centre, pending processing of our applications. Asylum seekers, refugees, illegal immigrants, boat people, call us what you will. We were all in the same boat, desperately trying to preserve our lives.

The Australian government planned to send four hundred of us to a small town in the Adelaide Hills, to live in a disused army camp. The local people were incensed. A meeting was called in the town hall. The mayor, local MP and police were present. Loud-mouthed hecklers were removed, but that didn't stop them spitting venom on the streets.

'Effing illegals! Why can't they go through the proper channels like we did?'

'Look at the crime figures. See the huge proportion of foreign names?'

'What diseases might they bring in?'

The meeting was called to order. The first speaker asked about security. Would they be imprisoned? What guarantees were there that they were no threat? Had they been screened for disease and criminal record? Parents were concerned about education, fearing large numbers of non-English-speaking children flooding the local schools to bursting point. There were insufficient doctors in the area, and the local hospital was now used as a geriatric nursing home.

The room stank of Nimbyism and xenophobia, but one lady claimed she'd be just as angry if four hundred Australians were evacuated from, say, a natural disaster, and placed there. The same problems would arise, except for the language issue.

One fellow of Italian descent pleaded that Australia had given him a second chance, a much-blessed life since he settled here after the war. He challenged the assembly to own up if they too were happy migrants. The room was silent, before many hands slowly crept up. Noticeably, the owners were people who had contributed positively to the local community, an asset to their adopted country. Someone interjected that the crooks and no-hopers wouldn't be at the meeting anyway, but he was countered by a lady beseeching: 'For goodness sake, where's your humanity? Give them a fair go. They've survived hell. When we came we weren't escaping torture and death!'

People began to realise the positives. There'd be work for locals, renovating the army camp. four hundred people need to be fed, and local stores would benefit. With some adaptations to the former hospital, medical care could be provided. Teachers would be needed, especially in English as a second language, and counsellors. It would not be necessary to overburden local schools, as not far away there was a recently closed primary school which could be used again. There would be risks and problems, but someone asked if any town was crime-free.

Miraculously, by the end of the meeting, most of the fence-sitters had been convinced, although the anger remained that consultation with the community had not occurred before it was a fait accompli.

So began my life in Australia. Valemount school was re-opened. All children of school age were sent there, to learn English without interrupting the education of local children. Preschoolers were taxied to local kindergartens, the government being aware that young children quickly absorb languages. The cost would be repaid by the saving on extra English lessons later. Soon, five-year-olds could be heard interpreting and negotiating for their parents in shops. After two years, those of high school age were gradually integrated into Wattlebank High, which by then was prepared for the influx. Some were now old enough to enter the workforce.

There were several doctors of our culture in the district, and one of them voluntarily transferred to our town. She spoke our language, and served only our community, in the re-opened hospital premises, not competing with the local practice.

I was one of those children who at thirteen went on to Wattlebank High. I had excelled in English, so the transfer went smoothly. I'd heard of compatriots in city schools being bullied and harassed, but at Wattlebank I encountered none of that, possibly because I have an aptitude for sport. I was selected for many school sports teams, and the state under-16 girls' basketball team. I ran for South Australia in 100, 200 and 400-metre sprints. My mother was concerned that I was neglecting my studies, but when I achieved three 20/20 merit scores for Year 12 exams and a tertiary entrance ranking of 97, she was elated. I went to Adelaide University to study a double degree in mathematics and computer science, also continuing my sporting interests and helping with an integration programme for newcomers in my own community. I passed with first-class honours, went on to do my Masters, and this year was awarded the Rhodes Scholarship. My younger brothers are now at university, one studying medicine and the other engineering. We are thrilled to see our mother so proud and happy, and grateful to Australia for our opportunities.

Not all my companions on that leaky boat fifteen years ago have such happy success stories, and indeed some did succumb to crime, resentful at the world for their horrendous past. Some have died following health issues arising from their terrible treatment in Afghanistan and on the journey here. I well understand the locals' concerns, and am doubly grateful to them for welcoming us, giving us hope and a new and happy life. I owe a huge debt to Australia, which I plan to begin repaying when I return from Oxford.

Fresh Start

Martin drew deeply on his cigarette, looking searchingly at his wife. He'd never smoked, but recently things were so bad, he said he needed the stress release. Helen said it only made things worse. He knew that.

'Things will have to change, Helen. I'm working all hours, so are you, we have no time for the kids or each other, the bills are piling up, we're always biting each other's heads off. Where in hell are we going?'

'You could lead the change by quitting the cancer sticks,' she retorted tartly.

Martin clenched his fists down by his sides. He loved her beyond measure but she'd driven him close to hitting her. He relaxed, and tried again to make her consider going to Australia.

'We'd be running away, and just what would we be running to? No family support, and what would we do for a living?'

'We'd be leaving the family's constant breathing down our necks, criticising in their minds even if they didn't say anything. Mechanics out there are paid much more than here, housing's cheaper, the whole way of life is easier. We can come back if it doesn't work out!'

'What about the kids, taking them away from family and school? Jack has just started high school, he'd have to change schools again. And Jodie has been picked for the county under-14 girls' soccer team. They'd be so resentful!'

'Kids mend, Helen. They'd see it as an adventure. Jack would have a breather before starting high school there. Soccer for girls is new there. Jodie'd romp into a team. Jerry will go to kindy and school before we know it.'

'You've got it all worked out, haven't you? What about me?'

'They're screaming for nurses, especially agency part-timers. Please, love, give it a go!'

She knew it was the only way to save their marriage. So began the form-filling, medicals, interviews, and research into this strange land about which they knew so little. These textbook meteorologists chose Adelaide as having the best weather. It also had affordable houses, an excellent health service, low unemployment, and was nestled between the hills and the sea. They were assigned to a flight on their wedding anniversary, three months away, allowing time to sell their house and possessions…and tell their family and friends.

The friends they still had after their troubles were shocked but supportive. Their mothers wept, said, 'How could you do this to us?' Helen's father came round and had a blazing row with Martin. Martin's father had a heart attack.

Martin called the emigration authority with the sorry tale, and they were granted a further three months to sort things out. They would leave in October unless they changed their minds. After a quadruple bypass and recuperation, his father was pronounced as healthy as the next man. Time now to broach the bogey subject again.

'Dad, we have to give it a go. We're not coping financially and…'

'I told you we'd help if you stayed!'

'That's not the answer, Dad. You and Mum have worked hard for your retirement, you're not going to compromise that for us.'

'We'd rather live like paupers and have you here than…'

'There's more than money, Dad. Jerry needs sunshine: you know he gets awful chest infections every winter. Jodie and Jack are so excited, we couldn't tell them now we're not going. We'd be back in the old routine, fighting, no money, so they can't keep up with their school friends. I couldn't bear it if we had to go through another incident like when Jodie started high school.' It was the first time that had been mentioned since Jodie stole a CD player from a classmate.

'You don't make kids honest by granting their every whim, Martin. You never had everything that opens and shuts when you were a kid!'

'Dad, this is taking us nowhere. I'm sorry, but we're going. We have to have a crack at improving our lives while we're all young enough. It won't be too long before Jodie has a boyfriend and will refuse to go!'

Martin left. His father wept.

On the journey to Heathrow, Martin and Helen were pensive. Jerry had never been on a train and was excited by all the new sights and sounds. Jodie tried to read but read the same paragraph over and over, taking nothing in. Jack was unaware he was irritating the other passengers by whistling in a low monotone while rattling a hand-held puzzle game. Helen decided it was time for the restaurant car. Over lunch, they would talk, allay each other's misgivings, calm their fears…maybe.

Heathrow was a nightmare. Helen wanted to turn round right then. A baggage handlers' strike had grounded all flights for twenty-four hours. The airport was almost fatally constipated. The backlog took forever to clear as flights were rescheduled, passengers shunted or rerouted. The children had severe gastric attacks, taking turns to vomit in inconvenient places. The airline put them in a hotel until things were sorted out.

Homesickness struck in Singapore. What have we done? We're only halfway but there's no going back. They tried to be interested in the wonderland of activity and colour…cable car to Santosa Island, dancing fountains, a plethora of exotic goods, so cheap, but it was all tasteless. They had nineteen hours to endure before their onward flight.

Australia at last! Adelaide, 15 October. The heat was reflecting off the tarmac, cooking them in their warm English clothes. People spoke English of a sort, but with hard accents. The airport staff were brusque. Passing through Customs was harrowing. Despite having nothing to declare, they were of course still subject to scrutiny, their luggage given the nit-comb treatment. But they were impressed by the thoroughness employed to protect Australia against imported infections.

An immigration officer met them and other new migrants, and after a lengthy briefing, herded them onto a bus to their temporary hostel. People were cracking with exhaustion after the long flight, children crying, one lady fainting. They took in little of the commentary as the bus drove around Adelaide. At the hostel they were well fed, shown to their rooms and left to shower and sleep. Next day began interviews, house-hunting, job-hunting. Many complained; Helen and Martin took stock.

'We've arrived safely, and at least we have shelter and food until we find our feet.' This, surprisingly, from Helen, who after a good night's sleep was feeling almost human. 'The kids are better, must have been something they ate. It's school holidays so if we hurry and find a house they won't need to start school in this area.'

'They'll have to stay here with you while I go to job interviews,' said Martin, 'and it's going to be a wagonload of fun house-hunting with three bored and homesick kids in tow.'

The family enjoyed getting to know other new migrants. There was a playgroup for Jerry and a room for older children to meet, read, watch TV or play table tennis and electronic games. They took a bus into town so Helen and Martin could take their driving licence exam, then Helen and the children explored the city and many parks while Martin attended a job interview. They bought a decrepit car for house and school-hunting, cheaper than renting one for a couple of weeks. The children enjoyed being allowed some input. Martin and Helen had wisely realised that they too had to live in the chosen location.

A new house was beyond their means, but they found a pre-loved home in a modest suburb, already equipped with carpets, curtains, and an established garden including orange and peach trees. The children settled into school, but Jack was miffed to have to attend primary school until the end of the year, because of the different school systems. Soccer had finished for summer, so Jodie had to be content with tennis, at which she also shone. Jerry went to kindy and would begin school the following February. Helen helped out in school; she knew that volunteering often led to paid work. All went well until…

Martin was made redundant at Christmas. The family were dumbfounded. 'But…why did they take you on if…? Oh, Martin!'

'Seems the country shuts down for Christmas. Everyone takes holidays or gets laid off. I'll have to go on the dole.'

'Dole! We've never had to do that! I'll get a job,' sobbed Helen.

'Not that easy, love, but you can try. I'll be a house dad, no worries.'

It was a shock to have to pay to see a doctor. The children picked up a swag of infections at school, and Martin almost severed a toe with the cranky lawnmower.

Their home had no air conditioning. Christmas was a miserable time. Their Christmas present to their families was an expensive phone call. A pile of cards and gifts made them weep…except Jerry, who wondered why they were all so unhappy. It was oppressively hot and humid. Tempers frayed. They went through the motions of Santa, gifts, Christmas dinner, with no heart in it. Martin wondered if it would always be like this.

Then, in the evening, a former workmate of Martin's called. 'How about coming to our place for lunch tomorrow? Bring your bathers, we have a pool. There's masses of tucker. My in-laws never made it,' he added with a wink and a grin, 'Just bring some beer. You'll be more than welcome.'

Stunned, they accepted. Such generosity to newcomers!

In February, Jack started high school. He was overwhelmed by the sheer size of the place, amazed by the lack of discipline and the insolence of his classmates, bored with the work which he'd already covered in England, and teased mercilessly about his Pommie accent and ignorance of Aussie rules football. His sister was no help; she loved school. Helen and Martin went to see the principal on Jack's behalf, and this was just the fodder the teasers needed.

'Oh, Jumping Jack's mummy and daddy came to see Grumpyguts Grimshaw. Poor little Pommie bastard's too clever for this class. What shall we do with him today, eh?' So the bullying started.

And Jodie, although winning popularity for her sporting skills, still yearned for more acceptance, and began getting involved in teenage peer group hassles – petty stuff at first, insolence to teachers, smoking, copying homework – but she was on the slippery slope and soon was drinking, experimenting with drugs, stealing again. The balloon went up one lunchtime when the yard duty teacher caught her in a dangerously passionate embrace with the school stud, at the far end of the oval. Martin and Helen were called in, and that was the end of Bradshaw

High. The family moved to the country, a reckless move before they had even sold their house. It cost them a year on bridging finance at an astronomical interest rate, which almost compelled them to return to Bradshaw.

But they loved their new circumstances. Martin could travel in to work, Helen was welcomed with open arms at the local hospital, and Jerry settled happily into primary school. Of course the students at the high school were flesh-and-blood normal teenagers, pushing the boundaries as always, the difference being that this school had effective sanctions, protecting both miscreants and those who did want to study. Jodie made it into the state junior girls' soccer squad, while Jack regularly achieved distinctions in nationwide maths and science competitions. Financially devastated though they were, the family had never been happier.

Through sheer hard work and habitual thrift, they climbed out of their monetary hellhole. When the time came for overseas travel and study scholarships, Jodie and Jack in turn were selected and able to go.

Jodie wrote home from Europe, 'I've met a lovely guy, a ski instructor in Switzerland. We're having a lot of fun. He's teaching me to ski but in case you're worrying, don't…I promise I'm being good.' She was, even if her definition of 'good' was not the same as her parents'.

She kept up a correspondence with the ski instructor when she returned home. He visited them the following European summer, when working as a rafting instructor near Cairns, and Jodie went to join him. Helen was correct when she thought she could hear distant wedding bells, fearing their baby girl would go and live overseas, and they'd see little of their grandchildren…

Jack's scholarship was for a year at a USA university, interspersed with work experience in the aircraft industry during vacations. He was offered, and accepted, permanent work at the end of it. Helen was bereft, and naturally became over-protective of young Jerry, now a strapping teenager.

'But Mum, you let the others!' was his justifiable argument whenever he wanted to spread his wings, at which point Martin would intervene on his behalf. Jerry soon learned he could always have his heart's desire, as his parents desperately wanted to keep him in this country.

They succeeded in the worst possible way. They bought him a car for his seventeenth birthday, and soon came the phone call every parent dreads. Jerry was in intensive care following a head-on crash into a tree. Unconscious, he could not be breathalysed, but he had a blood alcohol reading over twice the limit. Fortunately no one else was involved. Over time, he recovered partially, but would never join Jodie on the ski slopes or achieve his dream of being a pilot.

Helen and Martin were relaxing on the patio, watching the sunset, orange juice in hand. They could never stomach alcohol again after Jerry's crash.

'Penny for them!' teased Helen as Martin looked pensive.

'I was just thinking over our lives, the hard times we've had. Do you have any regrets about coming to Australia?'

'Absolutely none. We don't know what hard times we'd have had in England. We've survived, and look now: Jodie and Jack happily married, four lovely grandkids, the wherewithal to go and see them, which gives us an overseas holiday too. Jerry's courting a lovely girl who loves him despite his disabilities. We're healthy and happy with lots of friends. We even managed to bring our remaining parents out for a holiday. My mum said, "We love you, we miss you dreadfully, but now we're glad you came. Don't come back, things are very bad at home, you're better off by far here. And we're proud of you for allowing the children the freedom to explore and enjoy their world." I told her we had no choice, they were only doing what we did – moving on to improve their lives. I did say, however, that we were grateful for *their* attitude and loved them the more for it. It's quality time together now, rather than quantity. Ironically, the closeness with them is even stronger. Like the old saying, "Absence makes the heart grow fonder."'

Martin took her in his arms and his wordless hug spoke all necessary volumes.

Cuckoo!

Lois and Frank Jefferson had enjoyed a long, warm summer evening in the garden of their farmhouse, and had retired late. Soon it would be harvest time, when every daylight hour would be spent at work.

They were not pleased, therefore, to be awakened at four a.m. by the relentless cuckooing of the bird of the same name. Frank flew out of bed and grabbed his air rifle to fire a potshot out of the window to scare it away, when he was arrested in mid-flight by strange sounds in the lane. Voices carried on the still air, and he quite clearly heard, 'Don't do that. You'll bugger the battery!'

On hearing the car being cranked with an old-fashioned starting handle, and a reluctant sputter from its engine, he decided he was not going to oblige with the loan of a tractor to pull it off, and returned to the warmth of his bed. Within seconds, however, there was a scuffling in the front porch and loud hammering on the door.

Frank and Lois tore downstairs and beamed a torch through a window onto the porch, where a young man lay, his hands covered in blood. Was he a victim, or a criminal himself? Of course they called the police, who promised urgent aid. 'Don't let him in!' the sergeant advised. As if!

But the man was bleeding profusely. Lois was shaking with fear and simultaneously worried she'd soon have a dead body on her doorstep.

'Frank, look, he's in no fit state to do anything. I think we should go down and attend to him.'

Frank looked at her. If things went pear-shaped, it would not be the first time that Lois's kind heart had got her into trouble. A keen environmentalist, she hadn't even wanted to scare the cuckoo. She'd converted Frank to realising that if he always wanted to farm, he'd better think long-term and not just for the fast buck, but look after the land for future generations too. Now she wanted him to let in a bleeding stranger at four-fifteen a.m.

'Love, he could be dangerous. Whoever he is, he was obviously up to no good.'

The moaning from the porch had stopped; the man was deathly pale and had passed out. Lois prepared clean water, bandages, antiseptic and put the kettle on, the automatic reaction of Yorkshire farmers' wives to any sort of crisis. Frank gave in and went to the man. As they were preoccupied with patching him up and bringing him round, it was a while before they realised the police had not arrived. A second call had the sergeant in a tizzy.

'But…we sent a car…I can't imagine…'

His radio crackled. His colleagues had found another seaman dumped in the lane. The man spoke no English and was terrified by the sight of the law. They were bringing him in.

'Yes, fine,' said the desk sergeant, 'but what about the farmhouse? There's an elderly couple frightened to death with a man bleeding on their doorstep! Get yourself over there pronto!'

Frank returned to Lois and the sailor, to discover this one didn't speak any English either. They gave him sweet tea and put Frank's overcoat around him. Frank kept his now-unloaded gun handy, just in case. Finally the police did arrive and took him away.

It turned out that a Norwegian ship was in town that night. The sailors had gone for a night on the town, girls and all, but were unlucky with the ones they picked up. These ladies had 'contacts', including Lois and Frank's coal merchant, no less, wanted for aggravated burglary. The girls' flat was his repository for all manner of stolen goods. The girls had led the seamen into a trap where they were robbed, assaulted and dumped. But for Lois and Frank's cuckoo and a recalcitrant car, they might have got away with it.

Darkened Valley

It was a silver autumn morning, sunlight radiating out from under glowering clouds relieved by pinks, yellows and washed-out blue. The hills bore witness to recent rain, myriad greens vying for attention after the crackly dryness of summer. Xanthorea punctured the view with their spears, like Zulu warriors in grass skirts. Redgum, bluegum and stringybark dominated the unfenced track. Metamorphic outcrops reared up at intervals. The valley below seemed sleepy, although bustling with winemakers, farmers, artists and shopkeepers, the whole infrastructure of a thriving rural community. Galahs, New Holland honeyeaters, corellas and a willie-wagtail informed their universe of our presence. Trees and grass rustled in the rising wind that drove the clouds faster, lending an eerie atmosphere. We paused to rest on a fallen bluegum, revelling in the landscape. I hugged a rock, feeling its rough texture, its solid permanence. I ran my fingers over the stringybark, stroking its furrows, wondering what creatures called it home. I buried my nose in a patch of damp moss, taking in its earthy smell, and tried to track the location of the tick-tick-tick of a grasshopper. Curious cattle, Holsteins and Herefords, strode purposefully to investigate us.

A heifer lay dead, an oversized calf protruding from her, ripping her apart, agony suffusing her face even in death. The cattle gathered around her, bellowing their anguish. The fetid aroma of the ill-fated heifer was a poignant reminder of our farming days.

The putt-putt throbbing of a tractor grumbled towards us. A stockman, ruddy-faced, weather-beaten, tough and invincible, had come for the heifer. We hailed him as he picked her up on the forklift. He didn't respond at first. As we approached him we were disconcerted to see he was crying, this strong man of the bush. We expressed empathy for the death of valuable stock and the loss of nine months' production time. We'd been there.

He wiped a blood-smeared hand across his distraught face. 'I'm sorry. My wife and I wanted kids but we lost a baby last year, full-grown like this calf here. There'll be no more.' He revved the tractor, wheeled around and drove off.

I wept, joy turned to grief by this worst of all losses. We took our bushwalks elsewhere for the remainder of that season.

We enjoyed a long-overdue wet winter, and the magic of spring renewal. The welcome rains produced excessive undergrowth, and as summer approached, firemen and farmers were worried. By January we'd stopped mowing our once-green acre, withered to scratchy sticks and barren patches. Evenings became a ritual of watering, and checking our bushfire preparations. Shrubs pruned? Rubbish cleared? Roof sprinkler operable? Tennis ball in gutter? My fire-fighter husband Jim and his crew were as prepared as possible, as the annual anxious anticipation began.

10 February. Extreme fire danger day. Hot winds from the north. Brigades on twenty-four-hour standby. Residents warned to plan ahead, decide early whether to leave or stay and defend their homes. The first call went out soon after 11am, smoke seen rising from the direction of 'our' bushwalk. We surveyed outside, detecting the odour of fire, acrid fumes mixed with ominous, prickly fear. Radio warnings advised that township residents were currently safe but should listen for future advice. We deemed ourselves sufficiently far distant to be able to stay.

The wind rose, as it does in a bushfire, cool air rushing in to replace hot air rising. The fire was taking on a life of its own. Wisps of dead grass carried on the wind to a shed containing drums of agricultural chemicals and fuel. When the shed exploded, embers catapulted skywards and were blown towards the nearest township. Residents on the valley fringes evacuated. Schools closed early. There were losses of sheds, fencing and livestock. Entire homes, wardrobes and bath toys, fridges and lipsticks, families' everythings, were reduced to molten jetsam, but with no loss of human life – yet.

Jim rang in from our local fire station. '"I'm going up there, love. They need reinforcements. It's a bad one. Don't know when I'll be home.'

I persuaded the children to go to bed at eleven o'clock, thankful that our eldest was safe in the city. An orange glow suffused the horizon to the north. The wind had changed. We could perceive the thunder and lightning of the fire even though it was still twenty kilometres distant. I wanted to flee, but the time for options was long gone. If this conflagration had us on its list we'd need to stay indoors until the fire passed, then get out before the roof caught alight.

The continuing news coverage advised that a burnt-out ute had been found in a paddock, its driver missing. An hour later, an update announced an unconscious man had been found, his name 'withheld until relatives had been informed'. He'd been trapped while trying to move stock to safer ground, a task which did not leave him the option of staying with his vehicle. Television newscasts showed 'our' bushwalk burnt out, paddocks bare save for stumps of grass trees and the twisted remains of fence posts and mangled wire. I mused how different it would be there now for Jim, from our idyllic walk last autumn. A darkness enveloped me as I remembered the stockman we'd met that day.

At three in the morning Jim walked in. 'We've been relieved,' he said, 'but I'm wanted back there in the morning.' He hesitated, but said no more.

I hugged him in his smoky, acrid-smelling, once-yellow overalls, now patched with black like a leopard. 'Jim, do you have to? They've found someone unconscious with not much hope.'

Momentary silence.

'Yes. As a matter of fact, it was me who found him. He's not expected to live.' He paused, hugged me tighter.

Without looking at his face, I knew he was fighting tears, wondering whether to tell me more.

'...and...Marlene, it was that farmer.'

I stiffened, feeling sick, then weak as my erstwhile throbbing pulse threatened to drop me in a faint.

'You don't mean...him?'

'They'd...he and his wife...they'd just found out she was pregnant.'

Further bulletins followed the man's progress closely. He was in a specialist burns unit with varying degrees of burns to fifty per cent of his body. I found out who he was, and we visited his wife at home.

"'He's allowed to have only me to visit,' she said. 'He'd managed to crawl to the bank of a dam and soak himself all over before collapsing. He's been in an induced coma since the fire, but he's conscious now. They're keeping him out of pain. He'll be badly scarred for life, but he's expected to live. Yesterday was wonderful, though. He squeezed my hand, and smiled a rather twisted smile because of his facial injuries, but he whispered one word to me: "Baby!"'"

Port Pourri

William and Millicent Chandler promenaded through the Port, aiming for lunch in a very special café after their cruise on William's beloved *Archie Badenoch*.

William had been instrumental in restoring the boat, originally built in 1942 as a supply-tender vessel for the Royal Australian Navy during World War II. When the war was over, *Archie* enjoyed a new life as a police launch, named for the first South Australian policeman killed in action. From 1946 to 1978 she saved many lives, being the only all-weather deep-sea launch patrolling these waters.

Willie and Millie had seen dolphins that morning, and vowed to take their grandkids next time they visited. They'd promised to take Corey and Tayla to the Maritime Museum, to see for themselves the kind of conditions William's great-grandfather had endured when he came as a free settler in 1880. They'd also see the lighthouse, and the anchor from Matthew Flinders' ship, the *Investigator*, and learn about South Australia's terrible shipwrecks. Some were still visible in ship graveyards along the Port River.

The Port had been Willie's life, Millie's too since they married. He still went every Sunday to help with the maintenance and running of the *Archie*, selling tickets on the quay, or commentating the cruise. They'd given him the day off for Millie's birthday. He was a volunteer after all.

They strolled past the courthouse. Willie smiled ruefully as he remembered he'd once appeared there, as a lad. His forebears were stonemasons, his great-grandfather had built the place, and there he was standing in the dock. Twenty-three years old though he was, he'd felt the end of his father's belt after that episode. Willie's mother had died when he was three years old, so he'd been raised by his dad.

'Just the two of us now son,' Will senior would say. 'You see you make her proud.'

Proud she would not have been to know her little boy had been involved in a drunken brawl over a 'lady of the night' who practised in the brothel housed in the pub on the corner.

'How many times have I warned you about them wimmen?' roared Will senior. 'They're filthy. You'll get the clap. There's plenty o' decent lasses looking for a worthy man with a trade to support 'em!'

In fact, Willie was rescuing the lady from a drunken mob of sailors fighting for her favours, but it all went horribly wrong and Willie was arrested along with the rest and hauled before the court. The lady's testimony saved him from a stretch.

But the beating was just the spur Willie needed to pluck up courage to tell his father he'd never wanted to be a stonemason. 'I'm going to sea, Dad,' he cried. All his young life he'd watched ships coming in and going out, loading and unloading, smelt the sea, heard the gulls, the waves, the chatter of men on the docks, and yearned to be part of all that the Port was about. All his adult life he'd reluctantly returned to his dusty tools and stone. Now was the time.

He landed a job on a grain-handling ship and left his domineering father to the stone bashing. Three years later he transferred to a ship carrying dolomite to the Port from a quarry up the coast, but after one trip, enter Millie. After one date he knew he would marry her, but she'd come at a price. He'd have to give up the sea.

'Just lookee at all them ships in the mud! Them ships' graveyards'll be your graveyard next, and when bairns come, what about them and me then, eh, Willie Chandler?'

'I can't go back to stone hacking. Too many painful memories,' he'd pleaded.

'Maybe we can get a little shop,' she'd suggested. 'This town needs a good grocery, or haberdashery, or even a café! We'll go into business ,Willie!'

So for forty years Willie and Millie ran Chandler's Café in a heritage building built by Willie's great-grandfather.

They had one son, David. Toddler David amused himself as best he could while his parents ran the café. Schoolboy David played outside in the street or was looked after by neighbours until the café closed. Teenager David was coerced into helping in the café during school holidays and weekends, so there ended his dream to play football for the Magpies. Fortunately he excelled at school, and determined to go to university, with a gap year overseas first, to find himself.

Willie flipped, paced the floor, fists clenched. 'You can't! What about the café? Me and your mum have slaved all our lives for you and now you just want to clear off across the world and leave us to it! NO, lad, that is just not on!'

'Dad, you ran the café for yourselves. It was because Mum didn't want you to go to sea, and you went to sea to avoid being a stonemason all your life. So now I haven't had that opportunity, because Grandad left that all to Uncle George. I wouldn't actually have minded being a stonemason, seeing my name carved in stone for eternity on some proud buildings like your courthouse. Anyway, I'm going. I've never been out of the Port for more than a day except when I went on the *One-and-All*. I'm a prisoner of this bloody teahouse!'

Willie knew it was true. He'd have to capitulate. He wept.

The rift might never have healed but for the intervention of another lady. David and Marie became engaged thirty years after Willie had the bust-up with *his* dad and ran off to sea. Of course Marie wanted to meet David's parents. At last David agreed, if Marie would make the first approach.

As soon as David and his parents saw each other, the tears began for all the lost years. Now they only look forward, as a new generation of Chandlers puts some light in all their lives.

Ring Ring

Laura Morcombe was dusting near the phone and picked it up on the first ring. She hated to miss a call, as you always had to ring the person back, and that cost.

'Hi, Mum. It's me, Connor. I've got news. Have you got a minute?'

'Why of course, love. I've got all day.'

'Well, Ashleigh and I are planning a holiday in America.'

'Ooh, that's great, son. Can Dad and I come too?'

Laura and Jim were perennial travellers but hadn't been to the States. Company was not what Connor and Ashleigh had in mind.

'Er, well, yes of course, Mum, but…look, Ashleigh doesn't know, I want it to be a surprise. I'd planned to propose to her at Disneyland.'

'Well, that's wonderful, and about time if I may say so. You've been living together for two years!'

Connor let that go. His folks were OK, good fun, in fact, and parents can still come in useful even when you're grown up. For helping with expenses, for instance. He'd persuade Ashleigh.

'We'll get together at the weekend to sort out an itinerary, but meanwhile would you go to my old wardrobe and look in the left-hand cupboard. There's an old pair of my work boots. In the left toe there's a little box in a velvet bag, wrapped in bubble wrap. I bought the ring a while ago and didn't want to hide it at our place.'

'Oh…er, yes, sure thing, love. Well, I'll have to go now. It's washday and I'm busting for the toilet. Great news!'

She didn't say, 'I have to chase the garbage truck, because I had a clean-out last week and your boots were in the bin. They're now rampaging about the hills, not on the end of someone's legs, but garbage-truck-powered.'

She hopped in the car and sped off. She knew the route and it wouldn't take long to catch them up on their stop-start journey, even though they had a couple of hours' start.

She arrived as breathless as if she'd run all the way. 'Stop, please, help!' She gasped out the tale of woe.

Greg and Max, the garbos, looked at each other.

'But Mrs Morcombe, they'll be mincemeat now, all compacted!' Greg said.

'Please, I'll buy you a slab of beer! It's worth a try!'

'Each?' asked Max, teasing.

'OK, each,' Laura agreed.

Max turned everything off and the three of them climbed into the back of the truck and started rummaging – yuk! Paydirt in ten minutes… maybe. A chewed boot…empty. After a further fifteen minutes, there it was, the other boot, mangled, but in the toe was a squashed box in a torn bag and inside, voila! The biggest, shiniest diamond ring Laura had ever seen. She cried.

Greg and Max grinned. 'Forget the beer, luv. Your face was reward enough. Made our day!'

'You can have a whole brewery if you'll keep quiet about this!' responded Laura, not altogether joking.

They were discussing the itinerary. Ashleigh wanted to go to Alcatraz.

'What the heck do you want to go there for?' said Jim. 'Pretty ghoulish. Remember how you freaked out in Tassie over the gory details of what they did to convicts on Maria Island?'

'Jim, ignoring it doesn't mean it never happened. It's history, and it fascinates me. You'll get to go where you want.'

Laura wanted to see the Golden Gate bridge in San Francisco. 'Wonder if you can climb it, like Sydney?' she said.

Connor wanted, of course, to go to Disneyland.

'Let's wait until we have kids to go there,' came from Ashleigh.

'We might not have kids, and we might not go back. Let's do it this time,' argued Connor.

'Where do you want to go, Jim?' asked Laura.

'I'll just go with the flow, but we have to consider how far apart places are. Think four air fares in between everywhere. Why not Alaska and Ushuaia?' he added sarcastically. 'It's all America!'

'We'll stick with middle USA, Dad, silly.'

So it was that they flew to Los Angeles, Connor with the ring tucked into his wallet. Their wobbly geography had its first lesson when they arrived to find Anaheim – that is, Disneyland – was a two-hour taxi ride away, and the traffic was not like at home.

So star-struck was Connor, he left his wallet in the taxi, and it was half an hour before he discovered it missing.

Panic set in along with the expletives. Jim calmed Connor and rang the taxi company, who radioed the driver, still of course on his way back to LA. The driver returned but Jim had to pay for the extra run. Ashleigh couldn't say a word as she had left her camera in the taxi and hadn't missed it until it turned up with Connor's wallet. Connor was so churned up he decided the proposal would have to wait. Maybe at Alcatraz. That was where Ashleigh wanted to go, after all.

Alcatraz was a nightmare. Ashleigh was upset, depressed, preoccupied. Laura took her shopping as an attempt at an antidote, but Connor decided this was no place for the moment of their dreams. We'll try the Grand Canyon, if we ever get there.

They did get there – just in time for a bout of unseasonal foul weather. It rained, it blew, the temperature plummeted. Carried along by a mass of wet and windswept tourists bent on seeing one of the greatest gashes in the earth's crust, was no place to propose to one's beloved. They moved on to Las Vegas, but found nothing to inspire them. Think gambling or nothing, was their impression. Back to 'Frisco then. It would have to be the Golden Gate bridge.

'Frisco was a mess too. Ashleigh had no insulation, a straw in the wind, and she could not face going up onto the bridge, convinced she'd blow off. Connor was becoming frustrated. Would they end up home again without his popping the question?

It finally happened on a harbour ferry. Beautiful day, calm water, light breeze, stunning environment, a glass of wine. Laura tipped off the crew.

Connor drew Ashleigh close, lost his tongue, then his carefully prepared proposal poured out in a rush, his legs shaking. 'Ashleigh, will you marry me? Here, look, I got you a nice ring!'

One stunned Ashleigh. One curious boatload. One cheerful announcement over the PA: 'Ladies and gentlemen, if you would come up on deck, we have a young man who just proposed to his… fiancée, I guess she is now, sir?'

Ashleigh went crimson, the four hugged, the skipper came down and proposed a toast, everyone clapped.

Connor's love for Ashleigh was immense, so he'd bought the biggest ring he could find…far too slack for Ashleigh's dainty hand. But there was no way she wasn't going to wear it before she could have it altered. It sparkled all day, being shown off to half the population of San Francisco, until they were alone in their room that night. Ashleigh removed the ring and placed it lovingly on the vanity while she and Connor showered. She put on her most gorgeous negligee, bought specially for the trip, cleaned her teeth, let her hair down and put the ring back on. This first night she'd wear it to bed. As she applied night cream to her face, the ring slipped off…and straight down the handbasin drain-hole. She let out such a shriek, Connor thought there must be at least a mouse or a spider.

Now what? Connor was a plumber but he'd omitted to bring his tools. Also he was unfamiliar with American plumbing. With luck, it was probably stuck in the S-bend. Good job she didn't lose it down the loo or it would be in the city sewer by now. He briefly wondered what riches there were in the sewers of the world. He'd sleep on it. Despondent, they retired. No chance of a romantic interlude tonight.

Connor had a phobia about elevators. Even though they were on the fifth floor, he would always use the stairs. Next day, in the same hotel on his way down to breakfast, he encountered, on the third floor, a couple of maintenance men, complete with tool bags. He told the story. They looked at each other. This hapless tourist won't be back, he must have money to be here in the first place. We'll milk this for all it's worth.

'What's it worth?' asked Jaxon, a burly foreman with nicotine-stained teeth and a moustache, cigarette behind one ear and pencil behind the other.

'Well, quite a bit. My girlfriend and I just got engaged.'

'No, I mean, what'll you give us to try to retrieve it?'

Oh dear. Connor knew the USA was big on tipping, and also that for the time being the American dollar was worth a good bit more than the Aussie one.

'Er…how about fifty bucks…if you find it,' he ventured.

'Each?' tried Ted, Jaxon's offsider.

Connor blanched. After a long silence he offered, 'Fifty altogether for trying, fifty each if it's there.'

The men thought it was their birthday. 'We've finished here. We'll come up now before we start the next job.'

Connor flew down the remaining stairs to tell his family, breakfast forgotten.

Today's excursion would be delayed until the ring was found. Back up the stairs now, the family and workmen were already inside their apartment when he arrived. They watched anxiously as Jaxon and Ted dismembered the plumbing. That adventurous diamond ring was there – in the company of someone else's tiny gold wedding ring. There was no discussion. Jaxon and Ted gave them Ashleigh's ring, asked for their reward and pocketed the wedding ring. Connor made to protest.

Jim held him back. 'Just let it go, son. We're on foreign soil, we can't win, you've got your ring.'

On their second foray to breakfast, Connor reported the incident. Reception were delighted. A very wealthy Japanese businessman had reported the loss a month earlier and offered a substantial reward. Jaxon and Ted hadn't a hope. It was revealed they had been paid a substantial back-hander for their personal services during work time, and had tried to steal the wedding ring. They were sacked on the spot.

The Morcombes and the hotel would split the reward, which paid for the Morcombes' entire USA holiday.

Stuck in the Mud

It was five a.m. and dawn was just beginning to light up a watery sky around Tumbameena station.

Melody Gordon couldn't wait any longer to wake her husband. 'Brett! Brett, wake up, I'm getting pains.'

'Huh? What time is it?'

'Don't know but it's getting light. Brett, I'm getting pains. We'd better be going!'

'It can't be the baby. You're not due for another six weeks.'

'Brett, I'm sure it…oh!' as another pain gripped her abdomen.

Electrified now, Brett pulled on his trousers. 'You get dressed, I'll get the Hilux.'

They'd bought the vehicle in anticipation of their first child. They'd need a family car as well as a workhorse. It worked alongside their ute as well as doing ambulance duty in this instance. Melody struggled up the high step into the passenger seat, and Brett put the Hilux in four-wheel drive as they both fastened their seatbelts on the move.

For months they'd scanned the sky, watching for rain that never came. Now it had, not in spades but by the tankful. The paddocks were awash, their dams were full and overflowing. A creek that you would normally not even recognise as such was in spate, scouring its rocky bed with fast-flowing urgency. Melody figured it was a good job she had gone into early labour; much later and it was anyone's guess how long it would be before they could get out.

Brett engaged low range, stopped at the brink of the rushing water, told her to hang on and roared across. He didn't quite make it up the other side, which was being eroded at a frightening rate. One wheel was bogged in tyre-sucking, slimy clay. Revving would make the situation worse. Brett hopped out, the muddy water squeezing his gumboots. He reached up to the roof rack for his banjo spade and tried to dig out the wheels. The old sacks-under-the-wheels trick would be hopeless. He went into the scrub with his axe and frantically cut some saplings, spurred on by the adrenalin rush caused by the knowledge that the life of his wife and unborn child were at stake. The force of the deluge had almost freed some saplings, making the job easier. He forced them under all four wheels.

'Melody, love, you'll have to help. You drive, I'll push. She's in four-wheel drive low, just take it very steady in first gear. Turn the wheel a bit so we come out in a new track, not the ruts we've made. Pity we didn't reverse across.'

Grimly holding on, holding her breath to cope with the pangs, Melody drove, Brett heaved and strained against the weight of the truck, the water, the grip of the mud. Suddenly something gave and the truck broke free with a lurch that carried it up out of the creek bed, only to slew sideways. They could go no further, but were safe for now, out of the path of the raging creek. A week earlier their farm track would have had potholes filled with bulldust, that treacherous, unbelievably fine desert sand with the consistency of their mothers' face powder, that dry-bogs or overturns many a tourist.

Damon Coulthard turned up for work at Tumbameena at six a.m., looking for Brett. They'd arranged to do some maintenance together on the only tractor still in the yard. The spare part had arrived yesterday and in view of the welcome change in the weather, they knew they'd need it. He looked around, calling. No Brett. No Hilux. Tracks in the mud leading away from the station.

He approached the homestead, knocked, called out, 'Melody? Brett?'

Melody was usually out feeding the chooks at this hour. He knocked louder and went inside. They never locked doors. The house was eerily quiet. No sign of breakfast, every sign of their having left in a hurry.

Then the light-bulb moment. The baby! She's not due yet but… He ran for the ute, which he knew would not go far in the wet, but was four-wheel drive so would be OK for a while. He reached the overflowing creek and gaped in disbelief. Brett was signalling SOS, the tail lights flashing red towards Damon. Melody was tooting the horn and waving a shirt out of the window. Damon knew there was no mobile phone service at the station, but had noticed their radio still sitting on the kitchen bench. He signalled back, first with the horn and then with the lights, 'Will get RFDS', and fled back to the homestead. Even if he could have crossed the creek, he'd have been unable to achieve anything. No land vehicle was going anywhere in that torrent; their stock-mustering helicopter had no navigating or rescue gear and only one seat besides the pilot's.

'Brett, Brett!'gasped Melody. 'It's coming, the baby's nearly here, I can feel his head. Oh, Brett!'

Melody's waters had broken, all over the floor under the driving seat. Brett hastily cleared a space in the back of the Hilux among agricultural chemicals, star droppers, ropes and other farming paraphernalia, and spread fertiliser sacks and the spare clothing they always carried. He helped Melody lie down, loosened her clothing, cradled her head, trying to remember what they'd learned about breathing and pushing from online antenatal classes.

Suddenly the baby was there, a red and wrinkled little scrap with a shock of black hair. Brett caught him deftly in his big capable farmer's hands and began to cry as he gently cleaned him up as best he could with the remains of his shirt.

'Here you are, Mum. Brenton Oliver Gordon. For goodness sake give him a feed. Look how scrawny he is!'

With no energy for a play fight, Melody's usual rollicking giggle was reduced to a weak, tearful smile as she accepted Brenton and a hug from Brett. Brenton knew exactly what to do. He had his mum, his dad and his tucker. No problem. Melody, completely incapacitated, gave herself over completely to this wondrous creature who had landed in their lives with a squelch.

Brett, however, had to come to grips with their predicament while he still had a wife and son. He hadn't quite grasped Damon's message but knew he'd get help, somehow. The neighbours were similarly placed and too far away, but Damon would use the radio, currently their last link with the world. Thank goodness for the Rapid grid-reference-plate system. Damon would report their six-digit number and the RFDS helicopter would know exactly where to come. He wouldn't be able to land but it would surely be easier than winching shipwrecked victims out of a wild sea, routinely managed by navy pilots.

Soon Brett heard the best sound of his life, the approaching chop-chop of whirring helicopter rotors. He climbed unnecessarily onto the roof and began to wave, bringing a smile to the faces of the pilot and doctor. He scrambled down, took his son in his arms and handed him up to the doctor suspended in a harness above the vehicle. His gaze apprehensively followed them before he went to assist Melody up onto the roof. When she was safely inside the aircraft, he followed. They had nothing but literally the clothes they wore, yet they had everything: their lives, each other and their newborn son.

Brenton was happily sucking, musing on the possibility that he was the youngest person ever rescued by helicopter, possibly the youngest ever to ride in one, when there was a sudden yelp from his mother. Brett had his arms around her shoulders. Brenton was not amused by the interruption to his first meal and began to object. Melody grasped her abdomen with a terrified look in her eyes.

'Stay cool, Mel, it's only the placenta!' said Brett soothingly.

'Brett, I think there's…there's another baby!' This from the doctor with a triumphant grin as though it were his own.

It took another five minutes for Brenton's twin sister to arrive, destroying as she did so Brenton's notion of making the *Guinness Book of Records*. Brett and Melody were speechless.

The chopper chugged on towards the city hospital. The pilot joked that he was only licensed to carry two extra passengers and he hoped there wouldn't be any more. Thrilled though they were, so did Brett and Melody.

As they approached the city they could see thick black oily smoke obscuring the buildings, and a little further away a sea mist rolling in, most unusual but a potentially deadly combination. A factory was on fire in the suburbs and the wind was having great fun with the resultant smog. A radio message ordered them not to land…as if! They could not see the hospital, never mind the reassuring H on its roof.

'We'll go to the nearest country hospital,' said the doctor. 'Your wife and the babies seem in good shape, the danger is over and there's really no need to go to hospital at all but after your adventure, I think we'll be on the safe side.'

'Time we introduced ourselves,' said Brett. 'I'm Brett Gordon, this is my wife Melody, our baby boy is Brenton Oliver, and we have yet to choose names for our daughter.'

'Mark Oliver,' said the doctor as he shook hands.

'And I'm his cousin Cromwell,' grinned the pilot. 'Geddit? Cromwell Oliver!'

'You've got to be kidding!' said Brett.

'Yes, it's Chris really but my parents have a weird sense of humour.'

'That's it!' said Melody. 'We had decided on Felicity for a girl but now her second name will be Olivia, for you two gallant rescuers!'

Brett's turn for a light-bulb moment. Felicity Olivia Gordon. How could he send his twins to school with the initials F.O.G. and B.O.G.?

The Motel

'Jordan, it's gorgeous here, but sadly lacking in decent tourist accommodation. Oh Jordan, why don't we build a motel? A real swanky job with spas and bars and a boutique and restaurant and hairdresser and swimming pool and…oh please, darling, what do you think? We'd make a fortune, the mountains and the river and the sea are already here and free, we could build a golf course…'

'Hang on, Jessica, have you the remotest idea what would be involved, what it would cost? For heaven's sake, girl.'

'Oh you, where's your ambition, your sense of adventure?'

'And where's your common sense? I know we have the money now the old man's gone, but…it takes for ever to get plans drawn up, get them passed for building then get it built, with inspections every step of the way, $400 please, every time. In any case, we don't need to do *anything*, we have enough money to live on for ever! And who have you in mind for the actual building?' His Adam's apple wiggled like it always did when he was aroused, and he flicked his greasy black hair out of his eyes with a characteristic shake of his head.

Jessica examined her long painted nails, as if she could read his thoughts in them rather than in his face. They ambled back to their four-wheel drive in silence, but the foundations were laid in their minds.

A university buddy of Jordan's was an architect, and she set them on a precipitous learning curve. So many permissions, so many rules, so many walls to climb before they laid the first brick. But Jessica had scaled the biggest one, getting Jordan to agree. The bank thought it was a splendid idea. Not that they really needed a loan.

Eventually builders arrived, six of them; truckloads of bricks on palettes, (oh, how Jessica had enjoyed choosing them, and the tiles, pavers, carpets, window treatments, furniture…) a cement-mixer truck, sundry shovels, wheelbarrows, trowels, and gradually the skeleton building, the beginnings of their dream, began to take shape.

A month into the project, the brickies called a strike. Jessica sulked, Jordan fumed. The plumbers did what they could at that point, but winter was encroaching and cement and water do not take well to being frozen. The work had to be put on hold until the strike was negotiated, the weather milder. All went well until the electricians found fault with the building when they wanted to install the wiring. Certain things needed amendment that Jordan's architect friend had not thought of, being mainly concerned with what she thought of as aesthetic design, never mind the practicalities.

Finally, lock-up stage. The glaziers had coped well with the fancy-shaped window recesses, the only casualty being a severed artery to an apprentice on the wrong side of a crashing pane dropped by his foreman. Paving was laid – the path to further riches! Telephone and internet connections were installed. The roof was adorned with slate-blue tiles, the finial on the gable the pinnacle of their dream. Three coats of paint were applied to protect against salt-laden breezes, and Jordan thought wryly it would last a bit longer than Jessica's daily personal anointing. Reverse-cycle air conditioning was causing problems, but two years after Jessica's initial brain explosion they had Stage One ready to go, a suite of ten rooms on the ground floor, all with en suite bathrooms, car parking and promises of utopic facilities to come. They began taking reservations for up to six months ahead, following extensive advertising on the internet and in local and international holiday brochures.

At last the first guests arrived, twenty people in a coach too large to pass through the fancy archway to the courtyard around which the rooms were clustered. Jordan and the driver carried the guests' suitcases to their rooms. Jordan and Jessica had to accommodate the driver in their own home, not having allowed for him as a guest.

After extensive advertising in the national press, they'd employed the best chef obtainable. With this profession sometimes comes the temperament of many artists, and on the first night he quit on account of insufficient ancillary staff, a disagreement with the butcher and a too-long hike from his domain to the dining room. The disconsolate Jordan went out for takeaway, times twenty-five.

Guests appeased at least temporarily, Jessica and Jordan became preoccupied with how to feed the next lot of guests. Fortunately these twenty were moving on next day, but a chef was needed for two private parties arriving then, as their own cooking skills matched their organisational flair. They called in a woman from the village, adept at egg and chips, hamburgers and sausage and mash, and made themselves mysteriously unavailable come dinner time. A dysfunctional lavatory in Unit 6 led to more drama, solved by Jordan's father. Conveniently, he was a plumber. They found him in the pub in the next town, still sober enough to do the job.

A woman in the second party declared she'd be completely unable to move on unless she'd had her hair done, so please where was the advertised salon?

'Mrs Callas, we did advertise that our salon would not be available until next year, but there is a very good hairdresser in the village. I can make you an appointment if you like,' offered Jessica.

'Oh, and how will I get to this place?'

'I'll drive you down.'

'Where's the nearest golf course?' demanded Mr Callas. 'There's nothing to do here while my wife gets her hair done.'

'I'll get Jordan to take you into Cambrook.'

That would take care of both Callases. The other guests would just have to manage for a while.

The internet connection was down in the entire district, and the phone rang incessantly during Jordan and Jessica's absence, more bookings being lost.

Jessica began servicing the remaining rooms when she returned, having primed Jordan to collect Mrs Callas after he'd dropped Mr Callas at the golf course. She discovered that a set of their spotless, fluffy brand-new towels now resided in a suitcase on the bus recently departed, and that someone had been violently ill during the night and left an unspeakable mess in the en suite. In another unit, the fridge had been fraudulently emptied of its cargo of drinks. The girl who was supposed to help Jessica had called in sick, and this on the very first day. Jessica's nail polish and temper were in a parlous state by the time Jordan returned with an equally unhappy Mrs Callas. So the nightmare continued.

There's a motel for sale near Cambrook.

The Real World?

It was a chilly six a.m. as Brenton Harland parked his Pajero at a vantage point to observe the *Spirit of Tasmania* sailing into Devonport. He was meeting Tamsin Banks, a cosmetics consultant from Melbourne who had worked for his wife Julie until the Harlands shifted to Tasmania. Julie loved the island but missed the hurly-burly, the glamour and social life of the cosmetics industry. Brenton had suggested she invite Tamsin over to help her set up her own franchise and consultancy in Deloraine, where the family were trying to establish a soft-adventure eco-tourism business.

The stately ship pulled in with a hoot of its horn, and soon allowed egress of vehicles – mostly four-wheel drives, necessary to anyone desiring access to the island's vast wilderness. Brenton scanned the small group of vehicle-less passengers, and soon spotted Tamsin, looking 'bandbox' as ever, not as though she'd spent the night at sea. Glossy brunette chignon, red jacket, black tailored slacks and handbag, and shoes to send a shiver down a podiatrist's spine. Bet she hasn't brought any bush adventure gear.

'Hi, Tamsin. Welcome to Tasmania!' Brenton greeted her with a hug, taking her suitcase. 'How was the voyage?'

'Pretty good thanks, Brenton. Bit rough in the middle but OK. How's the family?'

'Fine. Scott's preparing for a canoe expedition this morning. Fiona's gone to Hobart for the weekend, and Julie was still asleep, but I can make breakfast! Hop up into Red Dog and let's be off.'

Love of his new life poured out of Brenton as they drove to his home. 'The island is one-third wilderness, the rest a rural idyll except for Hobart and Launceston. There are problems, but the islanders have diversified ingeniously. As the economy cripples one primary industry, they find others. I bet some of your beauty products contain our lavender, and our cheeses and wine are everywhere. Logging old-growth forests is a political football at the moment and rightly so – logging means jobs and a huge boost to the economy, logging means loss of habitat and a huge impact on the ecology when trees hundreds of years old are removed. We're trying to make a quid showing tourists the value of the bush.' He paused for breath.

Tamsin was horrified by the amount of roadkill.

'Yes, it's sad. Our roads are meant for slower driving than usually happens, and the critters have no road sense!'

They arrived at Platypus eco-Pursuits as Scott was taking a canoe down to the river.

'Hi, Tamsin. Good to see you. Nearly ready, Dad.'

'I'll take Tamsin up to Mum and be with you ASAP.'

Julie was up, cooking a hearty breakfast and preparing the canoeists' morning tea. 'Hi, Tamsin. Gimme a hug! Good journey?'

'Great, thanks, and Brenton has been telling me all about Tassie.'

'Not quite, he hasn't, but he'll try. I expect you'd like to change?'

That had not been Tamsin's plan, but a shower would be nice. She reappeared in T-shirt, slacks and sneakers, and helped Julie with the canoe trip's morning tea.

Scott came in. 'Someone's rung in sick, Tamsin. Would you like her spot?'

'What, canoeing? I've never tried before.'

'Time you started. You're all changed. Get your hat, sunscreen and repellent and I'll get you a personal flotation device and show you the tub. It's sink-proof but it's not impossible to fall out.'

He took her to a single kayak, a touring kayak 1, introduced her to the group and began the safety spiel and some basic paddling instruction. Then they were off, very quietly, awed by their surroundings: flat water, cool sunlit morning, birdsong, waterbirds fishing.

Suddenly a broad bill topped by two golden eyes broke the surface, followed by a shortish, thick black body. Scott had made no promises but had expected they might be lucky.

'Usually a platypus would scarper just at the disturbance of the water, but these are used to us now, we're just boring old humans. That's your reward for keeping quiet.'

When they climbed out to take morning tea on an island, Tamsin wobbled her kayak and ended up knee-deep in water, laughing as Scott helped her. *So she's not just a city slicker, she can laugh at getting wet and dirty.*

Over lunch, Scott said, poker-faced, 'I guess you and Mum want to get down to business this afternoon?'

Tamsin acquiesced politely.

Scott burst out laughing. 'Just joking, it's only your first day and you're here all week. Mum's coming with us for a bushwalk. Wanna come too? You'll be stuck here with Dad otherwise and he'll have you doing paperwork or fixing the tractor!'

Her shoulders ached from the unaccustomed paddling but, *as legs are used for walking, she should be OK.* 'How far are we going? I've never been up a mountain!'

'Well, we won't explore the entire Great Western Tiers this afternoon, just a twelve-kilometre ramble in the Meander Valley. We'll see how it goes. Meander Falls and maybe Split Rock as well. Very pretty but a bit steep.'

So was Tamsin persuaded, but twelve kilometres sounded a bit daunting. *She and Julie could talk shop and plan their week's travels around the island, as they walked.*

The day was warming up and Tamsin kept quiet about snakes.

'This one's a bit of a baptism of fire for an erstwhile non-bush-walker,' cautioned Julie.

But Tamsin remained undaunted. *How else can I get to spend time with Scott?*

The track was all uphill so there was little breath left for talking until a little plateau near the top.

'So how did you take to this life at first, Julie?' asked Tamsin, 'I'm in at the deep end, almost literally.'

'I love my men, and they are in their element. Fiona's happy too.

She's found work in Launceston and a boyfriend in Hobart. I love the outdoors but need my fix of city living. A franchise seemed a good way to go.'

They sat on a rocky bench for afternoon tea, Scott, Julie, Tamsin and six walkers all munching and admiring the view. There was a rustling under the rock and a metre-long tiger snake slid out from underneath. They'd all been told this was unlikely – the vibrations of their boots should send snakes packing – but nevertheless to wear long pants, thick socks and gaiters if possible. If a snake appears, keep still and let it go. On no account attack it. Tamsin, terrified at first, stifled a scream and sat, fascinated, mesmerised by its black shiny beauty and movement. She relaxed and revelled in her second wildlife surprise that day. The snake went about its business and so did the group, to Scott's congratulations.

All went well until they were about a kilometre from the vehicle. Julie suddenly went down in a hidden hole, falling awkwardly. Scott heard the crack of breaking bone. Fortunately one of the group, Jedd, was a paramedic and made the best use of Scott's first aid kit. There was no mobile coverage but Scott had a radio telephone in the vehicle.

'Tamsin, would you stay with Mum, please, and Jedd, you're the best one to patch her up. I'll run back to call help. The rest of you please follow me and stay together but don't hurry – we don't want any more spills.'

Jedd took a walking stick, padded it with spare clothing and bound it between Julie's legs. They made her as comfortable as possible, supporting her legs. They had no painkillers other than a little paracetamol which she took with minimum water, realising she would probably be anaesthetised at hospital.

Scott was back in half an hour, breathless. 'The ambulance will be at the end of the track very soon and the paramedics will arrive with a stretcher about twenty minutes later. Tamsin, will you go to hospital with Mum? I'll take Jedd back, meet the ambos and debrief the group. I'll bring Dad to see Mum and pick you up.' Brenton was not home, so Scott left a note. Whoopdee-do, I get to drive back alone with Tamsin.

The prognosis was not good. Julie had a cracked patella and sprained ankle. She'd be in hospital for a week, and not back on her feet for several more weeks.

As they drove home, Scott broached what was on both their minds. 'So what will you do for the rest of the week, with Mum incapacitated? Would there be any chance you'd stay and give us a hand? Maybe you could visit the hospital when she's up to it and talk shop there.'

Tamsin tried to keep the joy out of her voice. After all, this had come about through Julie's misfortune. 'Of course, I'll do anything I can to help. I'll call the businesses we'd planned to visit, and postpone. I'll come back another time.'

Scott grinned to himself. Every cloud…! 'Great, I was hoping you would. You seemed to enjoy the day?'

'Oh, Scott, it was wonderful. To see a platypus and a snake, to go canoeing and bushwalking, to experience first-hand and understand what gets you here – even falling in the river was fun after the first instant of panic!'

'You did well. I must admit, I didn't think you'd want to go. And you were amazing about the snake, and looking after Mum.'

'I'm a woman, multi-faceted, multi-skilled!' she laughed.

Brenton was back when they returned, and on hearing their story high-tailed it to the hospital, leaving dinner half-prepared. Hurray, we're on our own again.

'Oh my, I don't know what he's making, besides a mess, but can you sort it out?'

'Easy,' Tamsin replied. She made Brenton's beginnings into a hearty stir-fry.

Scott found a raspberry crumble in the freezer and introduced Tamsin to the wine supply. 'Let's eat,' he said. 'Dad will be forever, he'll get something. I'll put some music on. Do you like country?'

'Jazz mostly, but whatever.'

So began a long cosy evening until they both started to yawn. They'd met of course in Melbourne, but Scott was at uni, Tamsin working in an alien field to an outdoor Aussie bloke. Now they were surprising each other by the minute.

'Must hit the sack, another big day with visitors tomorrow. I'm not going to sentence you to a week's domesticity but you'll be needing a rest and to visit Mum, yes?'

'Yes, indeed.'

'But…I'll be free in the evening. There's a session with a National Parks ranger in Deloraine hall. I'd really like to go. Will you come? And can I take you out to tea first?'

I've been here about seventeen hours. I've paddled a canoe, seen a platypus and a snake, fallen in a river, climbed up to a waterfall, helped with Julie's accident… and…I dream I've found myself a husband…

Julie was feeling much better, and she and Tamsin indulged in girl talk – cosmetics, families, hot goss from Melbourne…and Tamsin revealed she had a date with Scott.

Julie hugged her, laughing and crying. 'So that's what you do when I break a leg. People used to say that to each other as they went on stage when I was in amateur dramatics, but I really did it this time, just so you could kidnap my boy!'

'Hey, Julie, it's only a first date…but we are getting along well. Yesterday was just…life-changing. I don't know if I can settle in Melbourne now. I'm beginning to love the bush in spite of myself, and you are doing such a great job educating city people. I would love to be part of it one day.'

At the end of visiting, Tamsin had to be asked twice to leave.

Scott drove Tamsin to the ferry. 'It's been a wonderful week, Scott. I don't want to return to the real world.'

'Tamsin, dear…' he said with a farewell hug and kiss, 'this *is* the real world.'

The Tall Poppies

Brion Braintree had had a difficult childhood. His father thought he was autistic, back when that was a synonym for retarded, but his mother understood him. She spelt his name that way because she'd wanted a girl, to call Briony after her grandmother. His father said he should have been a girl, convinced he'd grow up to be gay, although gay-as-in-happy Brion was not. He didn't even play football; all he wanted was maths puzzles and such. As his father disliked any activity involving thought, there was no interest through which to bond.

When Brion started school, other kids hated him. One thought he was God's gift to the maths class, until Brion arrived. Brion could do long division in his head, and enjoyed correcting the teacher. This other maths whiz also happened to be the class bully, so soon had his troops marshalled. School was a nightmare. The only thing that made sense to Brion was the beauty and order of numbers, their reliable, never-changing logic. He plodded along in everything else, and feigned illness when it was time for sport, further sealing his own fate.

In Year 3 his teacher spotted his genius, and entered him in a national maths competition for Year 7 students. He achieved a perfect score, even on the curly problems put in to separate the highest scorers.

Mother of course was ecstatic. Father grunted approval of this proof that at least his son was not retarded. The teacher arranged for Brion to do high school maths from Year 4, a special provision for his exceptional talent. Brion had to toe the line and do everything else with his age peers, but the bullying eased off, thanks to some swift footwork by the same teacher. He endured school, and winning competitions years above his age kept him sane.

Time came for university. He knew he had to pass Year 12 in a variety of subjects, not hide behind his genius in maths to get him through life. He'd done a lot of university maths at high school, but his school counsellor was worried. He needed a social life. The Year 12 formal held terrors for him; how would he find a girl to partner him, with his two left feet and hatred of social occasions?

He had a cousin almost a year younger. Maybe his mum would ask Aunty Maxine if Stella could go with him to this compulsory event.

Stella paled. 'Mum, I can't possibly go with that nerdy egghead!' she screamed at the suggestion she be seen anywhere with her socially-inept cousin, but in the end, to please Brion's mum, her favourite aunty, she complied.

It happened that Stella had an exceptional gift for languages. At the dance, each talked animatedly about their special field, safe ground for conversation, and found themselves enjoying each other's company, even dancing and going for a drink together. Stella was headed for a different university, but close enough to where Brion was to study maths, for them to meet occasionally.

Stella was a bubbly, confident and vivacious young lady, who had survived the chop-down-the-tall-poppy syndrome by also being good at sport, and just average at everything except languages. She had a lot of friends of both sexes, but no special boy. She did not want to become sexually involved for a long time yet; the boys, of course, did. She was an average looker, as was Brion, so they attracted no special comment when out together, which suited them both fine. She found him stable, quiet and unassuming, and if he was sexually interested he certainly didn't show it – maybe because they were cousins? Whatever the reason, they both felt safe with each other.

Stella was appalled that Brion had allowed his mother to choose his course. 'Accountancy? A bloody bean-counter? Brion,' she said heatedly, 'for goodness' sake, we're not talking about primary school arithmetic here, but real maths, the sort that designs rockets and makes cutting-edge discoveries! With your mathematical talent, what the hell are you doing studying accountancy?'

Brion mumbled, 'Oh well, Mum's always chosen my path. I didn't know how to say no, and it seemed like a safe career option. Now I'm here at uni, I know I can do more. Next year I'll enrol in a double degree, finish accountancy to please her, maybe do astrophysics or something.'

As expected, they excelled in their studies. The following year Brion was accepted into a double degree with recognition of prior learning exempting him from some units, and getting him onto a fast-track course in the sort of maths most of us have never heard of. For the first time ever, Brion got excited about something. He called Stella with the news, and to arrange a celebratory date.

By now they were such firm friends, so comfortable with each other, they hugged warmly when they met – and this time both found themselves stirring, partly from the euphoric excitement of Brion's news, but something subtly more than that. Brion was the perfect foil to Stella's exuberance, she the catalyst that had awoken Brion socially – and now at last, sexually.

This raised issues. As first cousins, should they marry? If they did, should they have children? It was not illegal, but…

Brion's mother and Aunty Maxine decided, fearfully, that in these circumstances, they should divulge the family secret they had held close for nearly fifty years. They were not full-blood, first-degree siblings. Maxine had been conceived 'on the wrong side of the blanket' as they used to say, by a different father, though the same mother. That made Brion and Stella only half-cousins. Several medical tests later, they threw away their misgivings. They'd marry, and if children came they'd be delighted. If not, they were complete.

Children did come, twins, who turned out even more gifted than their parents. Julian's forte was the humanities, Chantelle's, science. Themselves a gift, they were gifted with parents who understood, because they had been there.

The Telling

I pulled up outside Grandma's house as I always did after school on Thursdays. I walked up the driveway more slowly than usual, agonising yet again over what I would say.

'Hi, Gran. How are you today?'

She looked at me steadily. I had a creepy feeling she already knew. She hugged me, I think more firmly and for longer than usual, then, 'I made some of your favourite lemon pie. The kettle's boiled ready. Come and talk to me in the kitchen.'

Oh hell. She knows. She'll still love me, but she won't approve. She'll tell me I have to tell Mum and Dad. And she'll ask what Matthew thinks, and ask if he knows. I know she's fervently against abortion, but what else can I do now Matthew has disappeared?

We chatted about inconsequential things – school, netball, had I seen *Red Dog*? (As if.) I nibbled my pie, had a sip of tea.

'And how's Matthew?' The usual question sounded loaded today.

'Fine,' I lied, and changed the subject. 'How's Sweep?' Her black cat had been to the vet's last week and she couldn't make him take his pills.

'Oh, he's fine now, thanks.'

A long silence which I couldn't fill and she chose not to.

'OK, Julie, what have you really come to tell me? Something's not quite right today, is it?'

Silence as I slowly lost the battle with tears.

'Oh Gran, I'm so sorry. You'll hate me, I've let you all down, I've let myself down, I just couldn't help it and now…' as I broke down.

She leaned forward, took my hands in hers and tried to meet my eyes. 'Is it…are you pregnant, dear?' She let me cry, shaking, unable to look at her, then eventually, 'Do Mum and Dad know?'

'Not yet.'

'What about Matthew?'

'Y-yes.'

'What did he say?'

'He s-said I'd better g-get rid of it…my baby…'cos we're too young to get married and we're still at school and I should have been on the pill and…oh, Gran…it's just too awful, I don't know what to do…

After the most unbearable silence of my life she said, 'How far on are you?'

'I've missed two periods.'

Another silence.

'You do need to tell Mum and Dad, Julie. Of course they'll be hurt, but trust me, they won't throw you out.'

'Will you…will you come with me…please, Gran?'

'Of course. The sooner the better. How about you hop in the car and we do it straight away? It'll only get harder, the longer you leave it. Anyway, what does Matthew think?

My turn to be silent. Thirty interminable agonising seconds elapsed as I tried to screw up more courage to tell her.

'Grandma…Matthew has dumped me. He won't come with me to tell Mum and Dad. He hasn't the guts and he doesn't want to know. And they've always said, if I get into this situation I have three options. I can have an abortion, have the baby adopted or leave home. They've made it clear they're not going to start again with their grandchildren.'

'Yes, I know, dear. But…listen. I have something to tell you now, but you must promise never to let Mum and Dad know I told you.'

I looked at her, puzzled and expectant, and promised.

'Didn't you ever figure out that Mum was pregnant with Ryan when they got married? True, your Dad stood by Mum and they've made a success of their marriage, he didn't waltz off as Matthew has, but… do you see, they were in the same situation so they will understand. It's human nature, Julie, or our species would have died out! Of course it's wise to wait until you can make a home for a baby but…since when did humans ever behave wisely? Now come on, go and wash your face and I'll take you home now. Today. We have no time to waste. Ryan can come back later for your car. You need to make decisions and plans for your life and your baby's.'

I climbed into the passenger seat of Gran's little Hyundai, still crying.

'Do you want to stay at school? You could finish this year before the baby comes, maybe have a year off to care for him or her and study at home.'

'I don't know.' I thought of my career plans. They still weren't fixed, it would depend on my grades, but I wanted to do something environmental, travel around Australia working with flora and fauna, land or water management…marine biology if I got a high enough Year 12 score. I'd start off with a degree from ag college or uni. Now a new little life that did not ask to be here, was about to curb my big ideas. Matthew had recently talked of getting engaged at the end of Year 12 and having a gap year together, we'd be eighteen by then…but now…

'Grandma?' I'd stopped crying and begun to think through the thick fog that all but obliterated my brain.

'Yes, dear?'

'I know some adopted people who've been mostly very happy, except they have this ongoing, burning desire to know who they really are. And I know some who have broken their parents' hearts with their behaviour, and the whole family has been thoroughly miserable and screwed up. I know that can happen with natural-born kids too but…I don't know if I could risk that.'

'That's my girl. You're starting to think things through.'

We pulled into a lay-by a little way from my place. Grandma asked if I wanted to talk some more before we went inside. I was silent for a while before beginning to sob again.

I suddenly burst out, 'Grandma, I love my baby! I know that sounds ridiculous. This has blown my life apart and he isn't even here yet but… if it's humanly possible, Matthew or no Matthew, I want to keep him. I know it'll be hard, I know it was different for Mum and Dad 'cos they stuck together but…I've got to make a home for him myself! I can't bear the thought of killing him. I couldn't live with that. Oh, I wish I was dead, I wouldn't have made love with Matthew if I'd known what he'd do.'

She let me cry a while, then said, 'Come on, Julie. You can do this. And I'll be there for you, always.'

She pulled into our driveway, got out and tapped on the front door. 'Are you there, Natalie? I've brought Julie home.'

Mum's face fell, wondering what was coming next. I stood there, silently weeping.

'Julie, whatever's wrong?' *At least she's standing there, alive, and doesn't look injured or sick. Trouble at school probably. It's obviously something worse than not making the first netball team, she'd have found out about that today.*

I couldn't say the words. Mum made me sit down.

Gran said ,'Is Trevor in yet?'

'No, it's a bit early. Mother, whatever is it?'

'Julie has something to tell you. She's devastated and she knows you will be too.'

Oh no, not the same way fixed as we were, surely.

Mum sat down on the sofa next to me and put her arm around my shoulders.

I turned to her and wept into her chest. I could feel her heart beating faster.

'Mum…I…I think I'm pregnant…I'm so, so sorry.' More wracking sobs. I felt so much worse because my aunty and uncle desperately wanted a baby. They'd been married for years and it just wasn't happening. How could I ever tell them? They were another reason I couldn't consider abortion.

Mum hugged me silently as Gran looked on.

Dad walked in. 'Hi, I'm home. Now what does my ratbag mother-in-law want?' he joked. He'd of course recognised the car. He stopped in his tracks when he saw the scene. 'Natalie…Julie…what…?'

'We've got a crisis, Trevor. Julie thinks she's pregnant.'

He clenched his fists by his sides, lost all his colour, caught his breath. 'She's what? Wait till I catch that bastard Matthew. It had to be him.' *I hope it was actually, at least he's a steady boyfriend and not just any Tom, Dick or Harry that she's been hobnobbing with. My daughter!*

'I'm so sorry, Dad. I didn't mean to, it just…sort of happened. I don't know what to do. I don't want an abortion, I don't want to have him adopted. I didn't want to be pregnant, I wanted to do Year 12 and go to uni and have a gap year and a career and some fun before I even thought of getting married but now… Dad, I want to keep him.'

You should have thought of all that before young lady. 'What does Matthew think?'

Silence. Gran and Mum looked at Dad.

'Oh, don't tell me, he's disappeared. That'd be right, lily-livered jerk, gets my daughter up the duff then can't face his responsibilities. And you! What about all that sex education? Don't you know how not to have babies if you must go messing around?'

'Dad, I told you, we didn't plan it, it just happened, honestly.'

'Don't make out it was the first time. I've seen the look in his eyes.'

Mum to the rescue. 'Trevor, she's too upset just now to make any decisions. Let Glenys go home now. Mum, it was so good of you to bring her home but I think just the three of us need to be together to talk.'

I didn't want Gran to go but obviously they felt awkward, having put her through the same thing themselves. Gran gave me a kiss and squeezed my hand, saying it would all work out. I wanted to believe her. I knew it was up to me to make it work.

'Right,' said Dad, 'so what are you planning to do about this baby? We've told you we're not starting again with sleepless nights, teething, tantrums, nappies…and what happens later when another one *just sort of* happens?'

'Trevor! Don't be so hard! I'm sure Julie knows about…about us. I was only eighteen, remember.'

'Yes, and I stood by you and we made a go of it. This is different.' *But I remember how shattered Glenys was and she still helped us. Natalie didn't have a dad to get angry with her either. Or support her.* 'Oh, I don't know, I just don't know what to say. Get dinner ready, will you, love. I'm starving and not thinking properly.'

A strained silence pervaded the dinner table. Mum hastily made my favourite lasagne but I couldn't eat. Dad devoured the lot. I cleared away and went to wash the dishes, leaving them to talk. When the chores were done, they called me over.

'OK, Julie, now I'm fed and calmed down a bit, let's try to sort this out. You say you want to keep the baby. So what about school?'

'Gran suggested I finish the year – I'd only be seven months by December – then I could look for a flat. I could take a year off to look after him and maybe study some subjects at home part-time. When he's a year old, he could go into child-care and I could go back to school, then uni. By the time he's at school, I'd be qualified.'

'Now, hang on a minute. That all sounds a brave plan but it's castles in the air, Julie. Who's going to pay for this flat, and four years of child care? Do you imagine you could work *and* study *and* care for a child? Time for a reality check.'

Mum was gazing into space with her mouth open.

'Dad, people do. I want to do that more than I want to have an abortion or have him adopted. I'd spend the rest of my life looking for him, in crowds and on buses and everywhere. And if I study and work, he'll have an interesting mum and a future. But yes, I will need some help. There's still the baby bonus and single parent allowance. I know it's not fair, I got myself into this situation, but I need the welfare right now. In time I'll repay it in taxes and HECS fees like anyone else.'

We were all quiet for a very long time. Dad picked up the newspaper, pretending to read. Mum put the TV on, not taking anything in. My mind was a maelstrom.

Eventually Dad threw the paper down and said, 'Well, you seem to be getting it sorted, Julie.'

Then he came over to me and hugged me and for the first time in my life I saw him cry.

I experienced the first pains at three a.m. I smiled to myself because it was Sunday and raining, and my uncle who was a farmer said stock always chose to give birth at three a.m. on a wet Sunday. I went to knock on Mum and Dad's bedroom door.

'OK, love. Give us a minute. We're coming. You get ready. I'll ring the hospital.'

The sister in charge said I couldn't possibly be in labour because I was not on the February books. Well, bad luck, lady, this baby's coming, whether your paperwork is in order or not. We arrived at three-thirty. They showed Mum and Dad to a waiting room and put me to bed. I was having pains every fifteen minutes. They let Mum and Dad come to me. I suddenly had to go to the toilet and got there just in time as my waters broke. They got me back into bed. An hour later, Christie Elizabeth made her appearance.

Mum cried. Dad's face said, 'Wish it was a boy, but she's lovely.' I was too exhausted to care. But Christie Elizabeth was here, alive, well, and she and I were going to have a great future – together.

War Widow

'This is not a home and family, it's just a house with five people in it all pulling different ways. Why can't we be like other people?' Laura's daughter Olivia screamed at her.

Laura felled her with a mighty slap to her face. 'Get to bed, you insolent brat, and don't let me see you till morning. Just wait till your father gets home!'

'He is not my father!' Sobbing uncontrollably, pain and shock and hurt overwhelming her, Olivia crawled up the stairs. Her father would have understood; it would have been a home if he was still around. Gordon was so…so cold towards her. Not just wrapped up in his business…aloof was the word. Six-year-old Sylvia was his but not Laura's, baby brother Peter, now aged three, came from both of them, adored and spoilt by his mother, drawing his father's grudging interest and hopes. He'd be a great runner and footballer one day, and follow him in the business.

Laura had drawn the short straw. The deal was, love me, love my child, but it was all a bit one-sided. She'd refused to go to Canada with her lover after Bob died, when Olivia was a toddler. This is what she got in exchange.

Sylvia came in, ostensibly from playing outside, but in fact having watched this scene across a recessed corner of the house, where by an unfortunate arrangement of windows and the hallway mirror, she could spy.

Innocently, Sylvia smiled up at Laura. 'Is our Olivia in trouble?' she minced.

'Go and wash your hands and face ready for tea.' Bloody sneaky little bitch, how much did she see? Not that it matters. Gordon won't care; it's not as if it was his daughter I'd hit. Woodenly, she busied herself with the meal. She'd burnt the potatoes during the fracas with Olivia. Gordon would complain and say what a perfect cook Ethel had been.

Ethel. Six years engaged to her, no sex until they married, Sylvia a genuine honeymoon baby, no sex during the pregnancy. Sylvia was born at home and Gordon had taken a day off. Two days later he came home from the workshop for lunch to find it not ready. Ethel was dead in her chair.

Peter was a bundle of sinless energy, part of his mother's heart, an antidote to ongoing grief. For him at least she would love Gordon and tolerate Sylvia. Olivia would have to adapt. She was such a disappointment. 'Your father would be ashamed of you' was Laura's favourite barb, switching between stepfather and the deceased one as a threat, as the situation demanded. 'You're not wearing jeans. Your father would have said there's nothing a girl can do in trousers that she can't do in a skirt' and so on, ad infinitum.

Gordon and Laura made a pact when they married, the same as any other family of the day but with extra baggage. Gordon would bring home the bacon. Laura would keep house, mother the children, deal with their educational and medical issues, not spend any money without his permission, give him ham for tea and chocolate biscuits and still cope within the bounds of her meagre housekeeping allowance. And they'd be faithful to each other till death did them part.

It had all started when Bob died, his ship sunk by a German torpedo in his last port of call before home. Laura had vomited for three days, and when an ashen-faced young policeman with hat in hand knocked on her door, she knew. Her life might well have ended there, but for two-year-old Olivia, all she had left of dear Bob. She'd have to take housekeeping jobs where there would be a home for them both. There were sick elderly ladies aplenty, widows and spinsters from the First World War, who would love a little toddler around to cheer them up. Laura would be housekeeper/nurse/companion, and she and Olivia would have food and lodgings, Olivia, a surrogate grandma.

Gertrude proved admirable. The two bereaved women sometimes cried together for their lost loves.

'I never even…knew my Albert, if you know what I mean, dear,' Gertrude confided to Laura. 'You see he was killed before we were married. It's a sinful thought but how often have I wished we had…you know…just once. I've nothing left of him but photographs.'

Enter Ted, Bob's closest friend, who had avoided the war because of a limp, the lingering legacy of a motorcycle accident. He'd spent a whole year trying to track Laura down since she'd sold her house and gone out housekeeping.

'TED! What…how…oh, Ted, I'm so pleased to see you!'

Incredulous hugs, tears, introductions. The mandatory cup of tea was offered, coffee being too expensive unless you could drink chicory essence in a black syrupy substitute, and all of them being teetotal Methodists.

With Gertrude wistfully looking on, Laura and Ted chatted animatedly for over an hour, interrupted often by Olivia whining for attention. Who was this man who was making her mother smile again and mostly ignoring her? Gertrude eventually took the hint and removed the fractious child to the kitchen to read her a story.

Ted made his move. 'Laura…I wondered if…it's eighteen months now since…you know…and I wondered if…you'd come out with me sometime?'

Why not? She'd liked Ted and no one would gossip if she was seen out with Bob's best friend. Ted of course was doing the chivalrous thing, looking after his mate's widow. He took her for a meal in the local fish restaurant. That meant fish and chips sitting at a table instead of out of newspaper on a bench in the park, luxury indeed. The war was still not over. They went to the cinema, sitting bolt upright and being careful not to brush knees or contact any other part of each other's bodies, two lonely people who liked each other and had not known love for a very long time.

The rekindled friendship was progressing nicely. Gertrude did not disapprove of Ted but could see where things were going, and fretted. If Laura married Ted… Gertrude solved the problem by having a massive stroke, and it was soon obvious she'd spend her last days in a vegetative state in a nursing home.

Laura blamed herself. 'Ted, oh Ted, I'll never be able to replace Gertrude, she's been wonderful. She was upset about what would happen to her because of you and me. Olivia is distressed and puzzled. I don't know what to do but I know I'll have to find another job.'

He sat her down and took her in his arms. 'I've wanted to ask you for a long time but didn't know how. Will you…will you marry me?'

Silence. There'd never be another Bob. Was it fair?

'I've dreamed of going to Canada for years but don't think I'd have the nerve on my own. We could start a new life, just the two of us.'

Laura stiffened. 'Ted, that sounds exciting but…I'm sure you mean the three of us.'

Silence, then eventually: 'No, Laura darling. I do mean just the two of us.'

Laura screamed, pulled away, almost spat at him. 'Ted! You can't mean me to put Olivia in the orphanage! She's all I have left of Bob. She's my baby, my flesh and blood and his, don't you understand?'

'Laura, Bob would have wanted you to be happy. We can have our own babies. Step-parenting doesn't always work, you know. She's a sweet little girl but… Fresh start, clean break, what do you think, eh?'

She showed him the door, and spat between her teeth, 'What I think is how disgusting, how dare you insult me like that. Bob would be horrified! I thought we'd both found something but… Oh, get out, get out!'

Olivia woke up and crept downstairs, standing in the doorway behind Laura, sucking her thumb. 'Why are you cwying, Mummy? Is Uncle Ted going?'

Laura hugged the bewildered child. 'I'm…just upset because Nanna is very sick and…she won't be with us much longer, she's going to heaven. When people get too old and sick to have a nice life, God takes them. We'll have to find somewhere else to live, another old lady to care for. And Uncle Ted won't be coming any more.'

Her blazing fury gave Laura courage and energy. She flitted between jobs for two more years, then, scouring the jobs columns, found this: *Widower with baby seeks live-in housekeeper. Child not objected to. Impeccable references.*

Gordon Darnley was a village carpenter on the outskirts of the city. She wondered. How impeccable? But what was a man to do, left with a baby? Olivia was five years old now, and would unwittingly serve as a chaperone at the interview. Nervously she dialled the number. He would pick them up on Sunday, take them to see his home and meet baby Sylvia and his parents, who were helping him to care for her. His mother had objected, jealously wanting to have Sylvia to herself, but he'd warned her to behave herself when Laura came. Laura warmed to this poor man trying desperately to run a business and care for his undernourished and none-too-clean baby girl. More than that, she felt sorry for the child. They agreed terms and Gordon took her home.

'What do you think to that, Olivia? A new baby sister. I want you to call her daddy Mr Darnley until he says you can call him Uncle Gordon, all right?'

Not all right, but one does not consult a five-year-old about one's course in life. Olivia was a shy, well brought-up city girl, and suddenly had to go to school with all these…ruffians, she'd heard Laura call them. They teased her because she said please and thank you and spoke nicely, not with the local dialect. And being bright at school, very chubby and hopeless at games, sealed her fate.

When the snow came, she imagined she'd escape school, but a local farmer brought a tractor and trailer and all the children rode to school in the back, in their Wellington boots and raincoats. So began Olivia's conversion to being a joskin, a tomboy whose real father would surely not have approved. She learned to copy the speech patterns around her, and laugh and throw a snowball back when the school bully rammed snow down her neck. She was on the slippery slope to becoming a Disappointment. Nevertheless, Olivia's life went more smoothly until Laura delivered the news that she was going to marry Mr Darnley.

'…and then you'll have a new daddy. Look, Olivia, we're going to play a trick on Mr Darnley. When he comes home tonight, he'll get lost in the bedrooms. Sylvia is too big for a cot now. She's going to sleep with you in our room, and I'm going to share with Mr Darnley. And he wants you to call him Daddy now like Sylvia does.'

Enter Peter, very premature, only seven months after the wedding.

'Mummy, I know Peter grew in your tummy, but…how did he get in there?' Olivia was now eight and naturally curious about where this adorable but mysterious little person came from.

'God put him there, like God put you in my tummy when your dad was alive' had to suffice for an explanation.

Sylvia wanted nothing to do with Peter, except to give him a sly poke and make him yell when nobody was looking. Gordon had Peter kicking a football as soon as he could walk, and helping in the workshop as soon as he went to school. The girls were banned from the heady smell of fresh sawdust, paint and turps, the banter of Gordon's workmen, the buzz of the bandsaw that would take a finger as soon as a chunk of wood, but Peter had better start learning as soon as possible.

One day when Olivia was eleven, she walked in on a strange sight when she returned home from school. Mr Darnley was making grinning faces at the window and putting his tongue out at Mrs Wilton next door! She knew he often went to fix things for her because Mr Wilton hadn't time, but why had he jumped back from the window and shouted at her as soon as he knew she'd seen him? She'd have to ask Laura.

She found Laura sobbing in the lounge room. Tact was never Olivia's forte, but it was not the best moment to enquire about Gordon's strange behaviour.

Gordon was burying himself in paperwork in a futile attempt to avoid the situation when Laura burst into his office. The ensuing row was not a suitable sight for three bewildered children, Laura screaming at Gordon to go to hell and have his precious Mrs Wilton. But the mores of the day proved stronger; she'd promised for better, for worse, and what would the neighbours think? What effect would it have on the children if she left? Who would care for Sylvia, how would she support two children?

They went for their customary seaside holiday, a week of sunburn if they were lucky, sand in the picnic lunch, toes cut with metal toy spades, even worse fates if it rained, but once a year Laura insisted on getting Gordon away from his work…and Mrs Wilton. Penitent Gordon, who did not have a molecule of fun in his whole body and rarely opened his wallet, paid for ice creams, donkey rides and Punch and Judy shows. He even allowed the children to bury him in sand, but drew the line at dipping even his toes in the cold sea.

The boarding house was cheap, meals were provided and Laura didn't have to do any chores. When Gordon thought he might have endured the beach long enough to accumulate sufficient Brownie points, he said he had a headache and would like to return to their lodgings. Laura's relief was palpable to all but Gordon; even the younger children had picked up the vibe that Mum was tense and snappy whenever Dad was around.

'That's fine, dear. I'll stay with the kids while they're having fun.' She settled with her book to enjoy some peace, leaving the children to their sandcastles.

Soon Olivia asked if she could take Sylvia and Peter to play in a rockpool, hunting for crabs or whatever mysterious creatures they could find. Laura concurred and was soon dozing in the sunshine.

After a while, she woke suddenly to the sound of her name being called by a familiar voice. She thought she was dreaming.

'Ted! Oh…it can't be… Ted, how on earth did you find us? And what about Canada?' Laura whispered in disbelief. His limp was worse, and he was all dressed up in a brown suit and shiny shoes…for the beach? She glanced around and noted that the children were at the water's edge, but they'd be quite safe. Olivia had her lifesaving certificate; Peter had inherited his father's aversion to water and wouldn't go deeper than his ankles.

'It's taken a while. I missed you so much, Laura. Canada was hell without you. I had to come back but…are those other two children yours as well? Olivia must be about twelve by now.'

'Thirteen. Yes, she's at grammar school and such a help with the other two. Bob would have been really proud of her.'

'So…you…married again?'

She couldn't hold it in. She sobbed all over the startled Ted, about Gordon, Sylvia, Peter, Mrs Wilton, the whole bloody mess. On impulse, he got down on his knees by her deckchair, pulled her to him in a warm, close embrace. Laura hadn't felt so safe since Bob.

'Come away with me, Laura.'

'Oh Ted, you know I'm trapped, I can't leave the children and… *where are the children?*'

They scanned the beach, Laura's rising fear bringing up bile, her head throbbing. They ran to where the children were last seen.

Peter was running towards them. 'Mummymummymummy, Sylvy's in the water. Livvy's gone to pull her out.'

A supercharge of adrenalin sent the unathletic Laura and the limping Ted sprinting towards the water. Ted ripped off his suit and shoes, charging into the rolling waves as soon as he saw Olivia. It was not a particularly rough sea, but a retreating tide and a deep trough too near the water's edge had proved too much for unsuspecting children. Olivia was safe but frantically and tearfully searching for Sylvia.

'Take Peter home and get Gordon! Send someone to call an ambulance,' screamed Ted to Laura. 'Olivia's OK. We'll go on looking for Sylvia.' For some unknown reason, Gordon was already on his way back to the beach when they met.

'Gordon, Gordon, come quick, it's Sylvia…' She gasped out the tale as she dragged the white, shaking Gordon with her, Peter sobbing as he followed.

No time for pleasantries, not the best circumstances to meet Laura's suitor. But…the man was at least trying to save his daughter, the daughter Laura had allowed to die the minute he left them together. Oh why, why hadn't he learned to swim? Couldn't see any use for it. Now Sylvia was gone, gone for ever.

The three adults stood on the beach, glaring at each other, hate oozing from Gordon, anguish from Laura, hapless embarrassment, guilt and vicarious grief from Ted. Olivia was gallantly trying to comfort the distraught Peter despite her terror and exhaustion. Bystanders had gone for police, ambulance and the town lifeboat.

Sylvia's little body was washed up on the beach a mile further down, on the next tide.

After the funeral, the icy silence between Gordon and Laura was replaced by vitriolic recriminations. Gordon took solace in his work. Peter began to wet the bed and stammer. Olivia's school grades plummeted. Ted telephoned often, and damn the party-line eavesdroppers. In her devastated emotional state, Laura succumbed. There would be no reconciliation with Gordon. She couldn't handle the effects on her children of the whole sorry mess. In a weak moment born of not having a confidante, she sounded out Olivia.

'Listen, love. Sit down, I want to talk to you while Peter's in bed. That…that day at the beach when Uncle Ted came… He really did his best, you know, to save Sylvia. He loves us, you and me and Peter. He wants us to go and live with him. Don't answer me now, but I want you to think about if you would like that. I know you and Peter have been very unhappy since Sylvia died, we all have, but we can't change that now. We need to get on with our lives.'

Olivia was silent for a while, then, 'Would I still be able to go to the same school?'

'Absolutely. And Peter's not enjoying school, he's so much brighter than the village children. I remember the tough time you had starting school here. He would go to a new school, near yours in the city.'

Olivia flung her arms around Laura, sobbing. 'Oh Mum, Mum, let's do it! Let's go! Gordon has never loved me.'

Laura let the name go. She couldn't make her call him Dad.

Snag. Gordon would never let Peter go. His only child now, his son and heir who would take over the business one day and be a football hero like he would have been if he'd had the chance. And what would the neighbours think? Laura thought if Gertrude were here, she would have known what to do. Oh Bob, why did you die and leave us?

Of course Laura could not afford a divorce, would not go off with Ted unless married to him. Gordon, mindful of the expense of it, of what his parents and the neighbours would think, and of losing his housekeeper and his son, reminded her of the 'for better, for worse' bit and refused to divorce her. So they dragged on through life, shackled to each other – but Ted's invitation would not go away.

Laura came to accept that Olivia had been right, damn the child. They were not a family, never would be. Which would be the more wrong and harmful: to continue like this, or leave and live in sin with Ted? Would the stigma be worse? Olivia would have gone in a flash; she shouldn't have discussed the issue with her before she'd thought it through and now Olivia was even more unsettled.

Gordon came home for lunch one day, just as he had all those years ago when he'd found Ethel dead. This time he found a 'Dear John' letter. Laura had gone, taken the children, and was setting up house with Ted. She would let him have access to Peter, and send the boy to help his father during holidays when he was old enough, but not at age seven. She and Olivia did not plan to see him again.

Olivia went to her mother one day when Laura was sick in bed and Ted was at work. 'Mum…do you remember that day…that day when you hit me… I'm…sorry for what I said,' before she broke down in sobs.

'Oh Olivia, Olivia, I'll never forget that awful time. I've regretted hitting you ever since, and shouting at you like I did. You were so right, and I couldn't admit it. Things were bad between me and Gordon long before Sylvia died, and that was the last straw. Losing a child is the most dreadful thing that can happen to anyone, and we must always remember that and not judge Gordon too harshly. He's been through hell losing Ethel, then Sylvia, but we couldn't go on as we were, we needed to make a fresh start. Now, look at me. I promise we'll talk whenever you need to, but meanwhile, you're going to keep on being a good student and big sister, and I'm going to be a good mum and make a happy home for all of us. And if anyone at school says unkind things to you because Uncle Ted and I aren't married, you can hold your head high and tell them it's adults' business and none of theirs. And now will you go make me a cup of tea?'